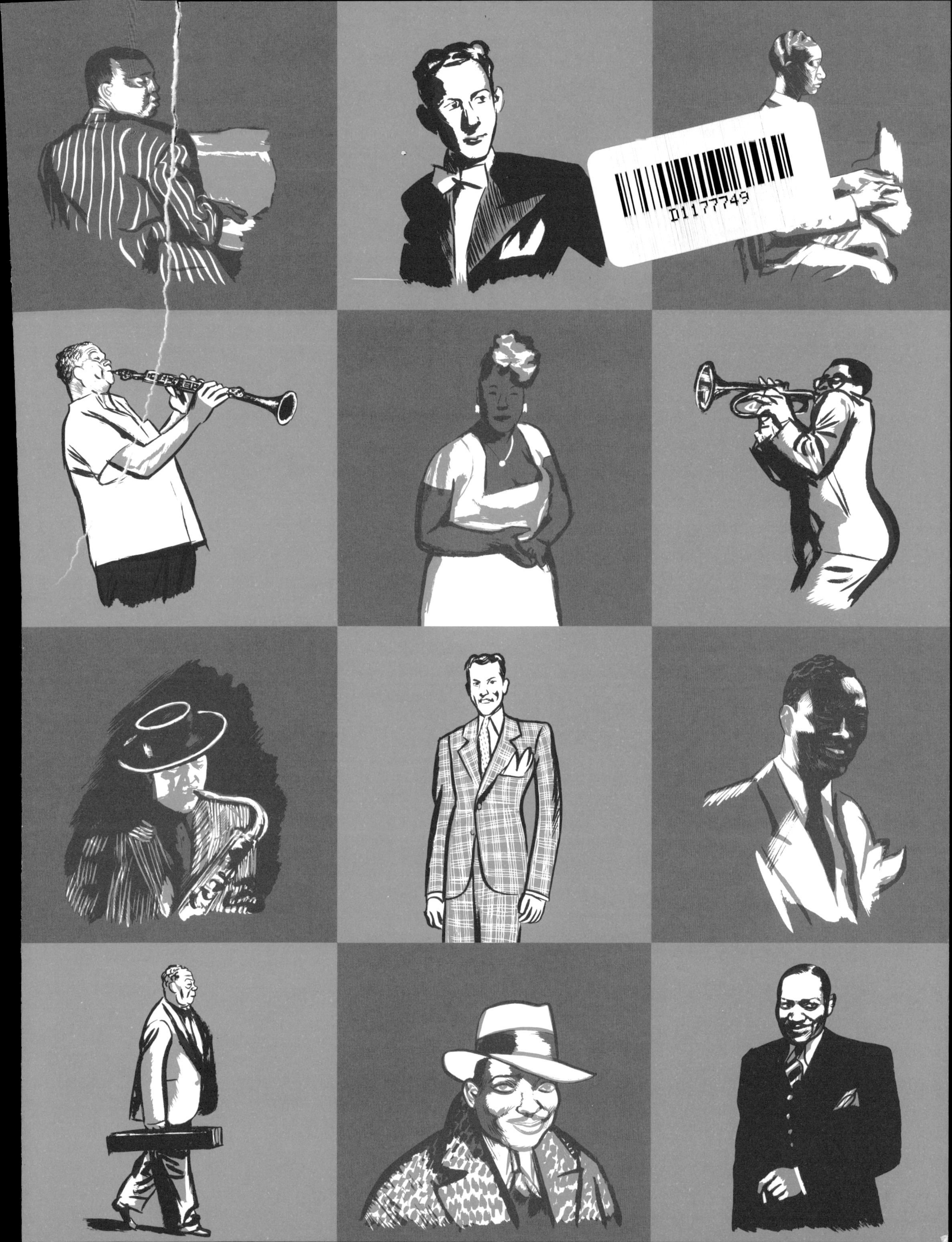

Translator: Barbara Appleby
Editor: Gary Groth
Designer: Keeli McCarthy
Production: Paul Baresh
Editorial Assistants: Gareth Bentall, RJ Casey, Avi Kool
Associate Publisher: Eric Reynolds
Publisher: Gary Groth

Cornelius Publications would like to thank the Big Band: Pierre Alengry, François Avril, Jean-Baptiste Barbier, Stéphane Beaujean, Sébastien Chevrot, Christian Druesne, Philippe Druillet, Frédéric Dubois, Alex Dutilh, Götting, Stéphane Labrosse, Michael Masson, Emmanuel Pollaud-Dulian, and Valéry Ponzone, without whom this book would not have sounded so good.

 Fantagraphics Books, Inc. 7563 Lake City Way NE, Seattle, WA 98115 (800) 657-1100 www.fantagraphics.com. Follow us on Twitter @fantagraphics and on Facebook at Facebook.com/Fantagraphics.

ISBN: 978-1-68396-086-7
Library of Congress Control Number: 2017950426

First Printing: February 2018
Printed in Hong Kong

BLUTCH
TOTAL JAZZ

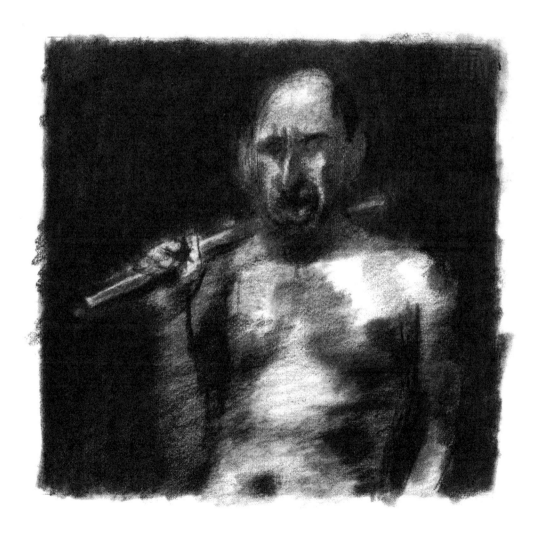

FANTAGRAPHICS

For Alex Dutilh

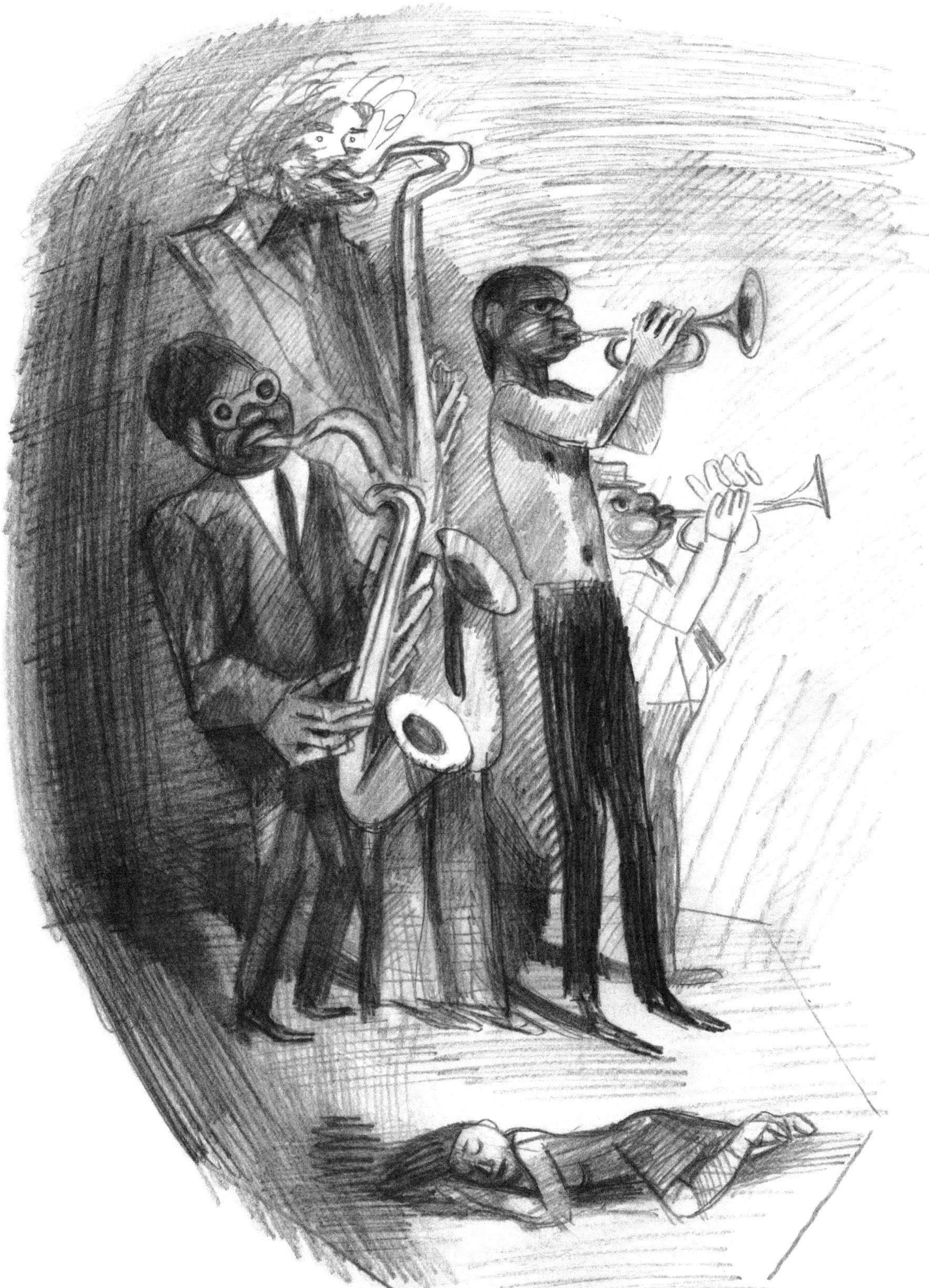

PREFACE

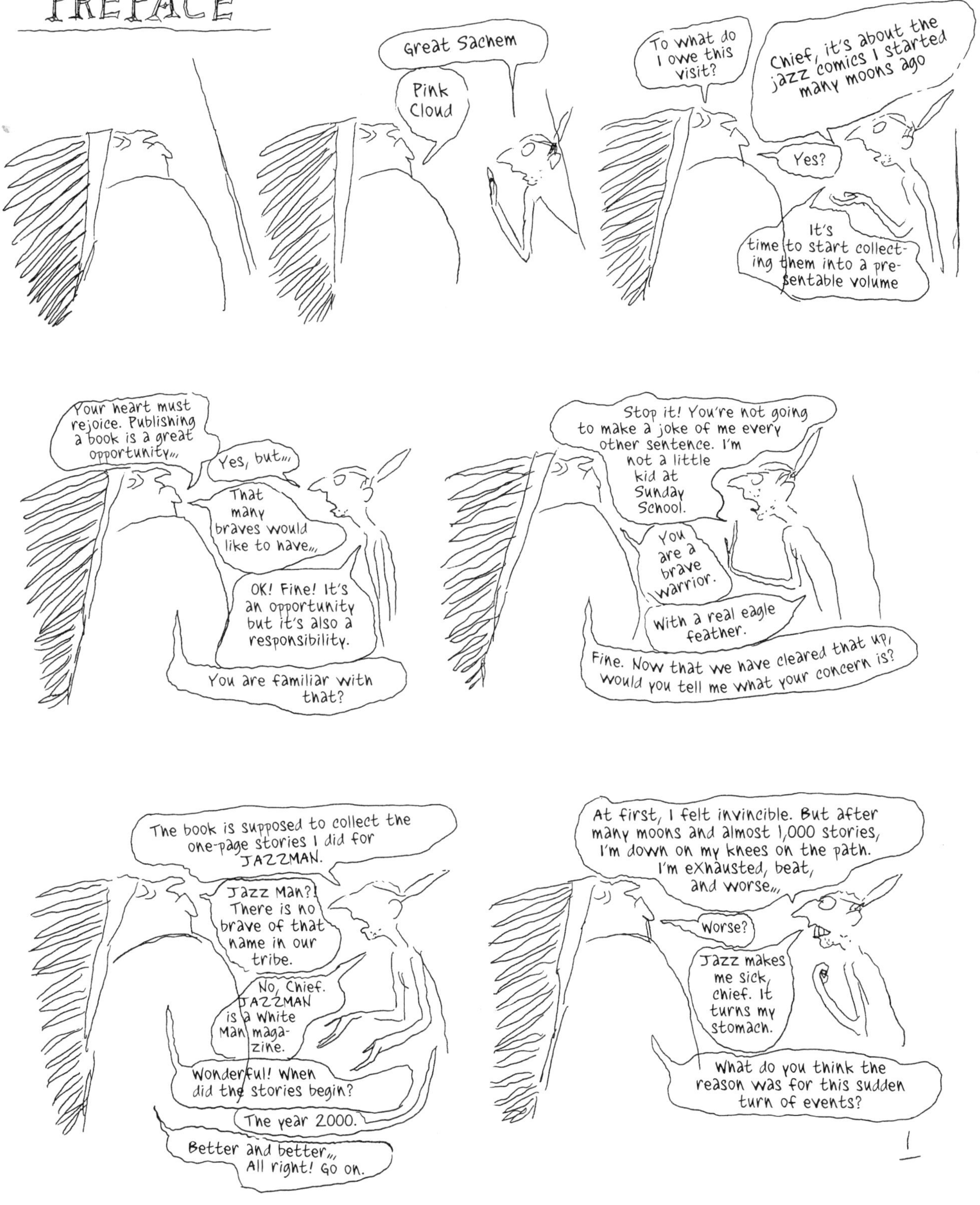

Great Sachem
Pink Cloud
To what do I owe this visit?
Chief, it's about the jazz comics I started many moons ago
Yes?
It's time to start collecting them into a presentable volume
Your heart must rejoice. Publishing a book is a great opportunity...
Yes, but...
That many braves would like to have...
OK! Fine! It's an opportunity but it's also a responsibility.
You are familiar with that?
Stop it! You're not going to make a joke of me every other sentence. I'm not a little kid at Sunday School.
You are a brave warrior.
With a real eagle feather.
Fine. Now that we have cleared that up, would you tell me what your concern is?
The book is supposed to collect the one-page stories I did for JAZZMAN.
Jazz Man?! There is no brave of that name in our tribe.
No, Chief. JAZZMAN is a White Man magazine.
Wonderful! When did the stories begin?
The year 2000.
Better and better... All right! Go on.
At first, I felt invincible. But after many moons and almost 1,000 stories, I'm down on my knees on the path. I'm exhausted, beat, and worse...
Worse?
Jazz makes me sick, chief. It turns my stomach.
What do you think the reason was for this sudden turn of events?

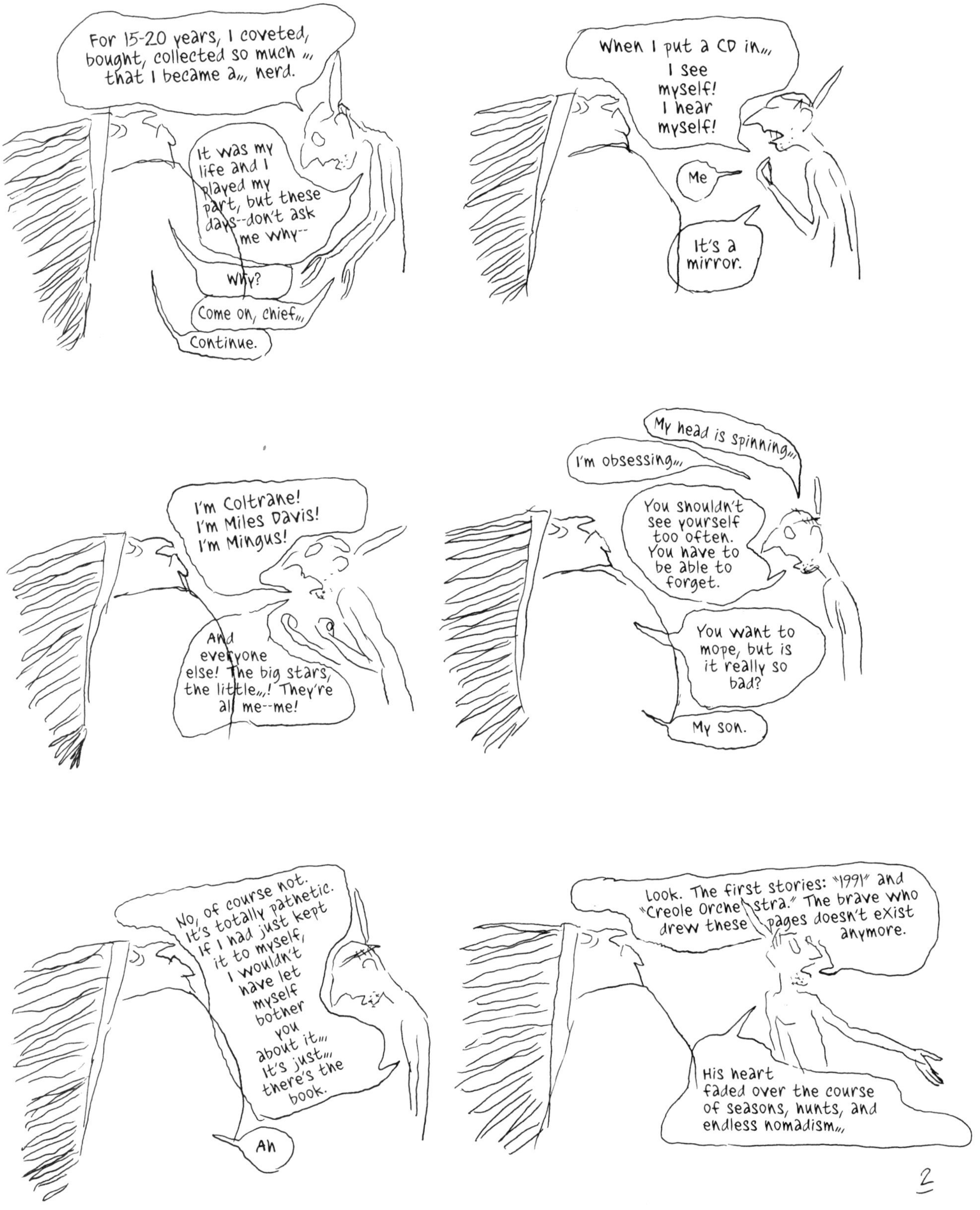
For 15-20 years, I coveted, bought, collected so much ,,, that I became a,,, nerd.
It was my life and I played my part, but these days--don't ask me why--
Why?
Come on, chief,,,
Continue.
When I put a CD in,,,
I see myself! I hear myself!
Me
It's a mirror.
I'm Coltrane! I'm Miles Davis! I'm Mingus!
And everyone else! The big stars, the little,,,! They're all me--me!
My head is spinning,,,
I'm obsessing,,,
You shouldn't see yourself too often. You have to be able to forget.
You want to mope, but is it really so bad?
My son.
No, of course not. It's totally pathetic. If I had just kept it to myself, I wouldn't have let myself bother you about it,,, It's just,,, there's the book.
Ah
Look. The first stories: "1991" and "Creole Orchestra." The brave who drew these pages doesn't exist anymore.
His heart faded over the course of seasons, hunts, and endless nomadism,,,
2

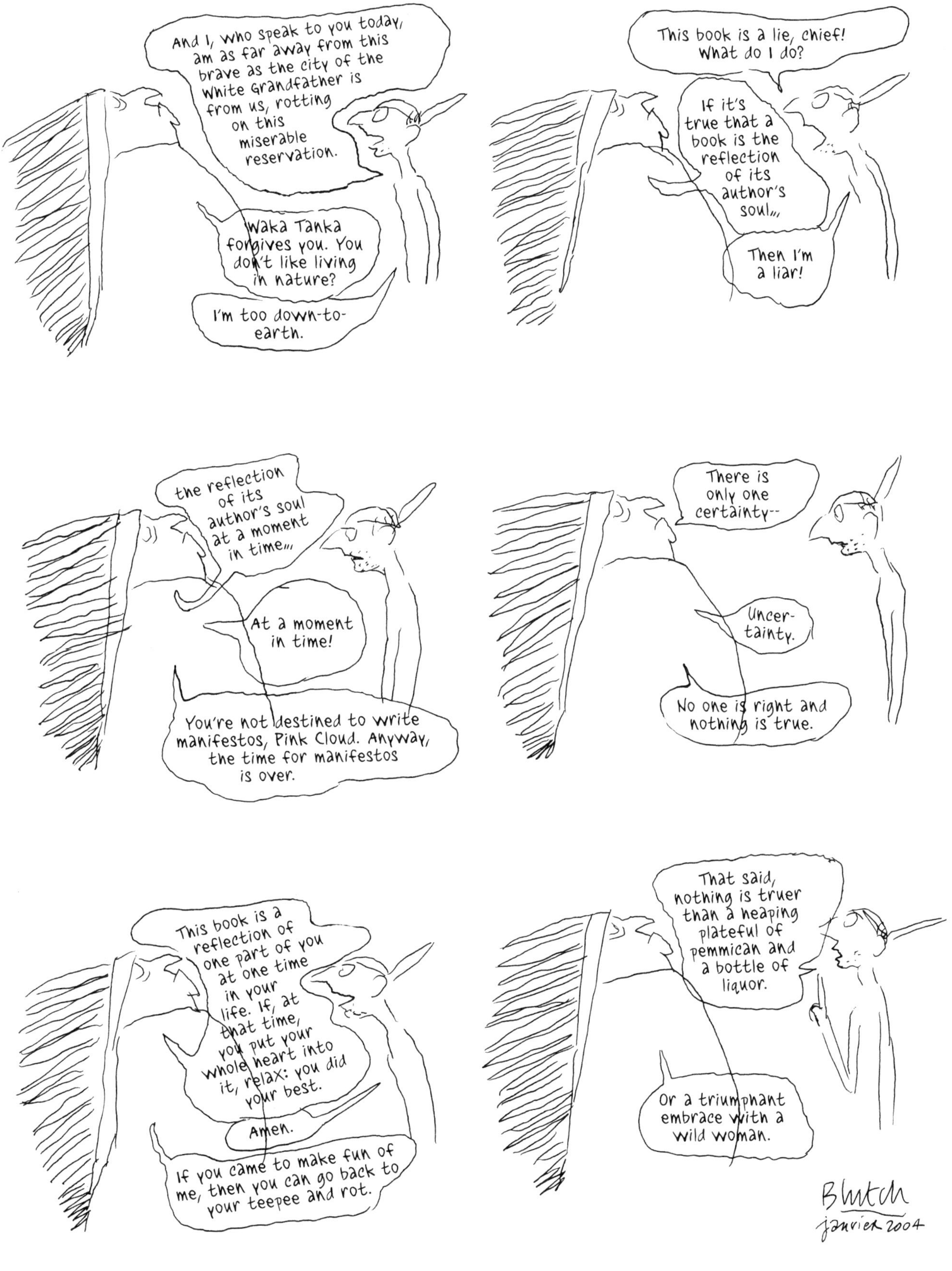
And I, who speak to you today, am as far away from this brave as the city of the White Grandfather is from us, rotting on this miserable reservation.
Waka Tanka forgives you. You don't like living in nature?
I'm too down-to-earth.
This book is a lie, chief! What do I do?
If it's true that a book is the reflection of its author's soul...
Then I'm a liar!
the reflection of its author's soul at a moment in time...
At a moment in time!
You're not destined to write manifestos, Pink Cloud. Anyway, the time for manifestos is over.
There is only one certainty--
Uncer-tainty.
No one is right and nothing is true.
This book is a reflection of one part of you at one time in your life. If, at that time, you put your whole heart into it, relax: you did your best.
Amen.
If you came to make fun of me, then you can go back to your teepee and rot.
That said, nothing is truer than a heaping plateful of pemmican and a bottle of liquor.
Or a triumphant embrace with a wild woman.
Blutch
janvier 2004

warning

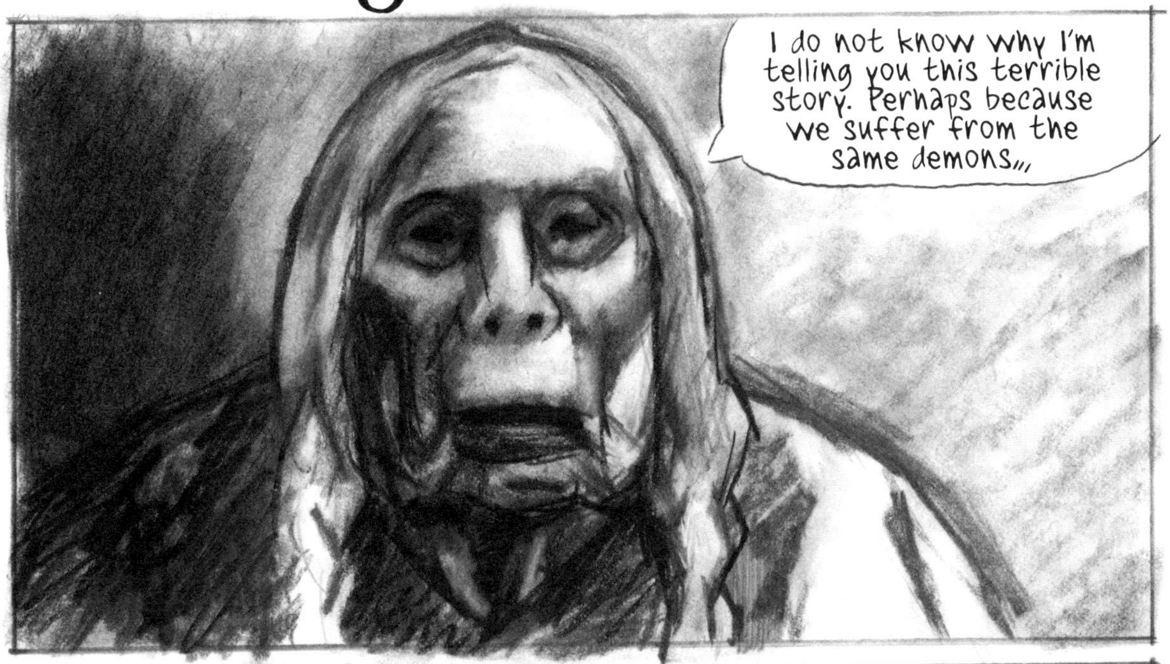
I do not know why I'm telling you this terrible story. Perhaps because we suffer from the same demons...

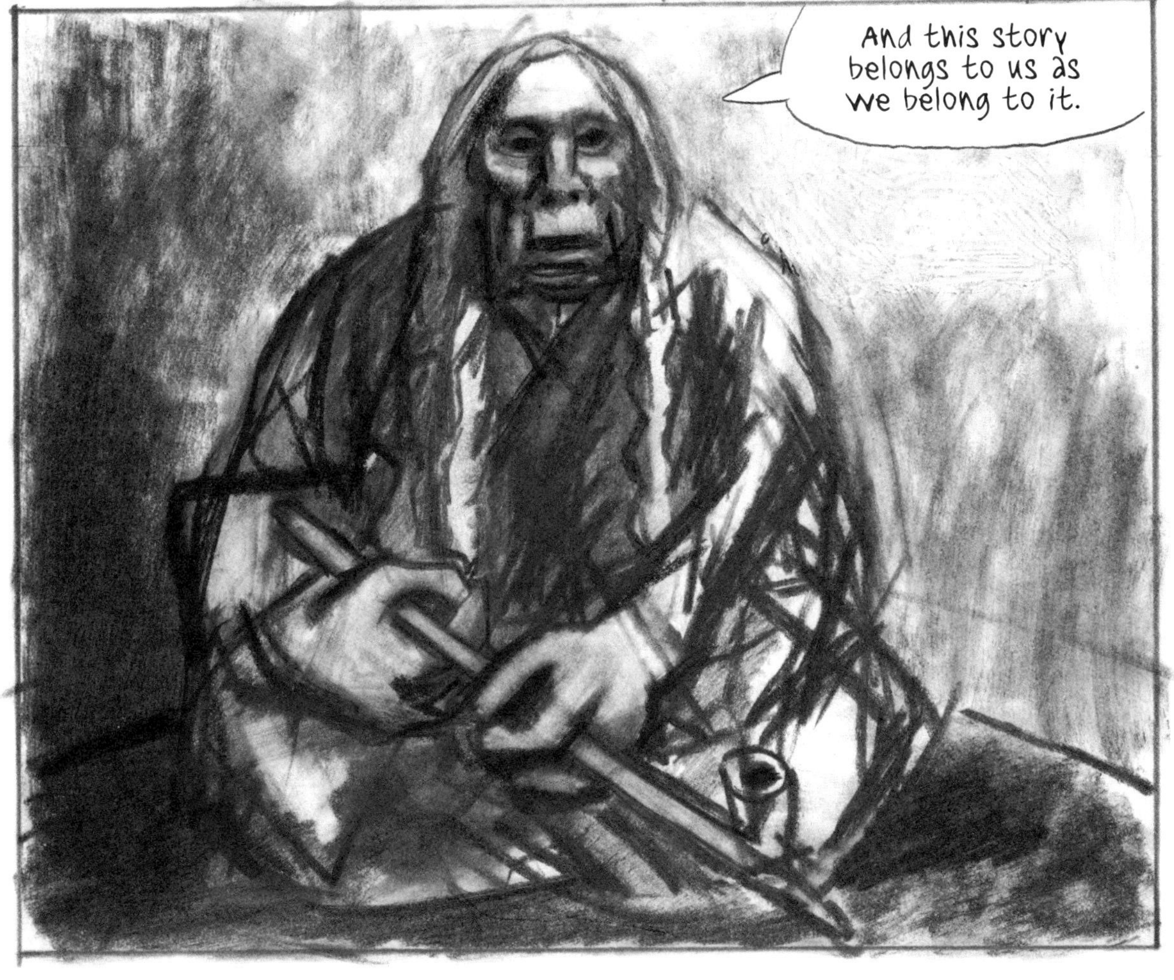
And this story belongs to us as we belong to it.

the Melody of Words

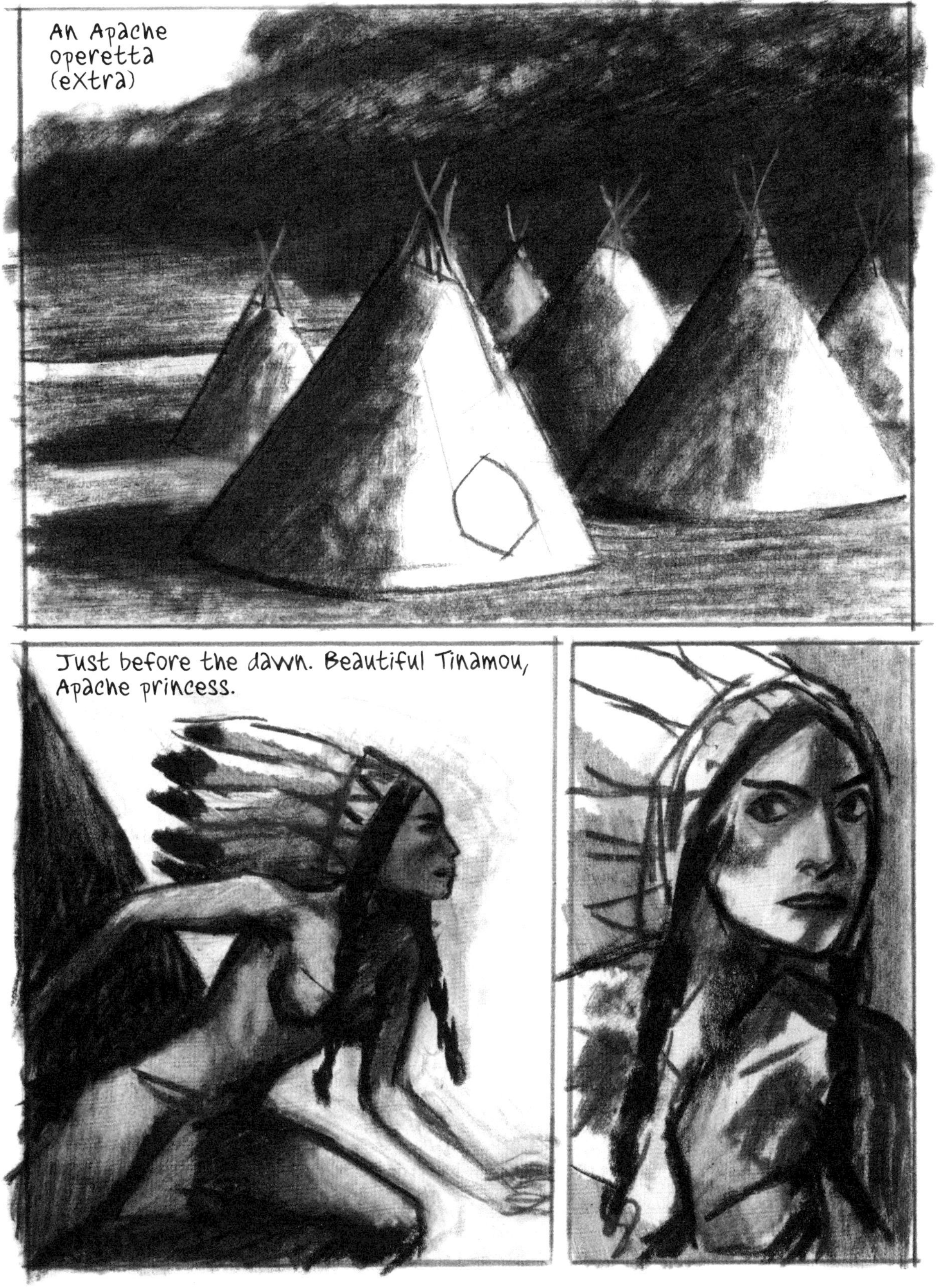
An Apache operetta (extra)
Just before the dawn. Beautiful Tinamou, Apache princess.

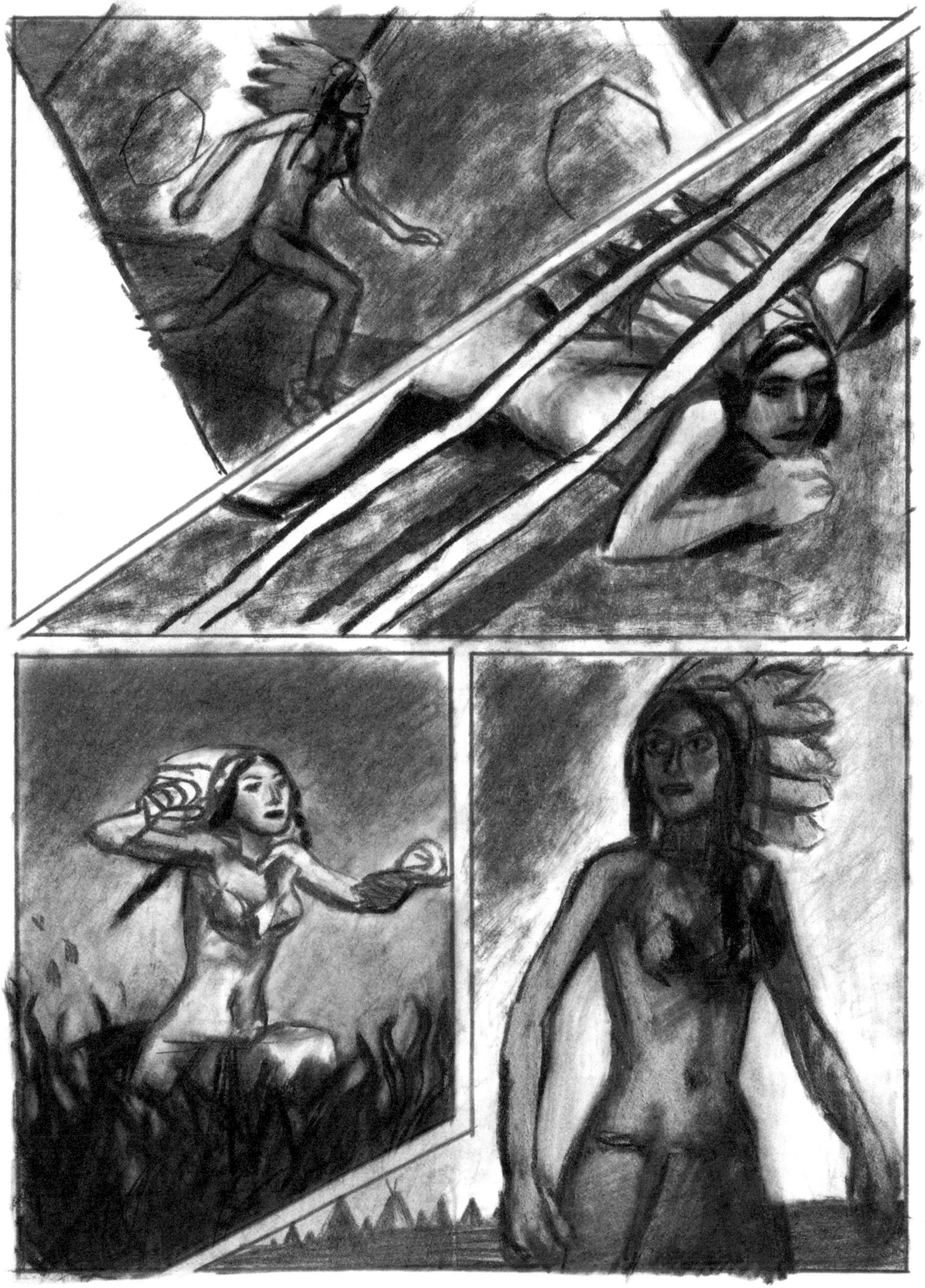

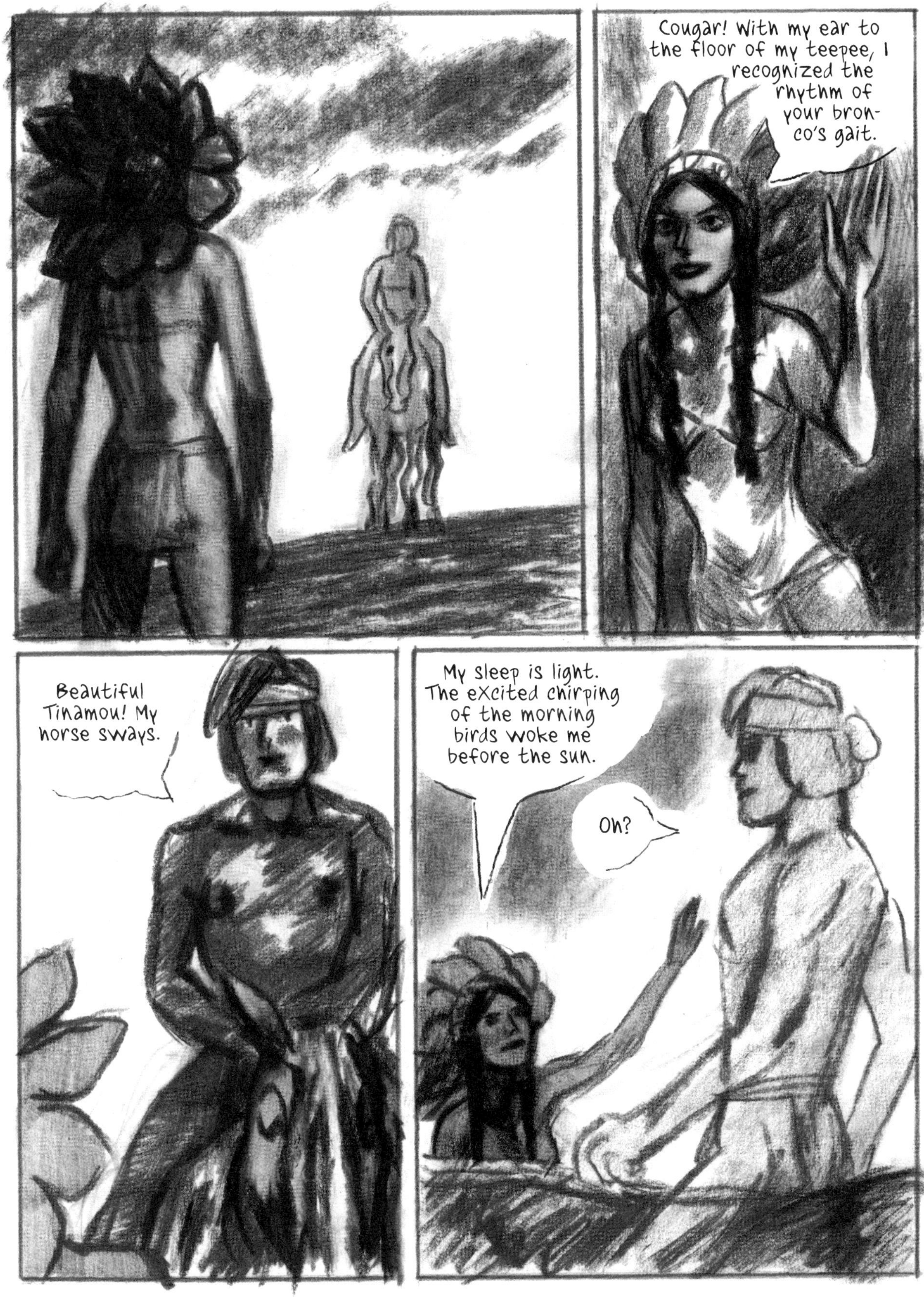
Cougar! With my ear to the floor of my teepee, I recognized the rhythm of your bronco's gait.
Beautiful Tinamou! My horse sways.
My sleep is light. The excited chirping of the morning birds woke me before the sun.
Oh?

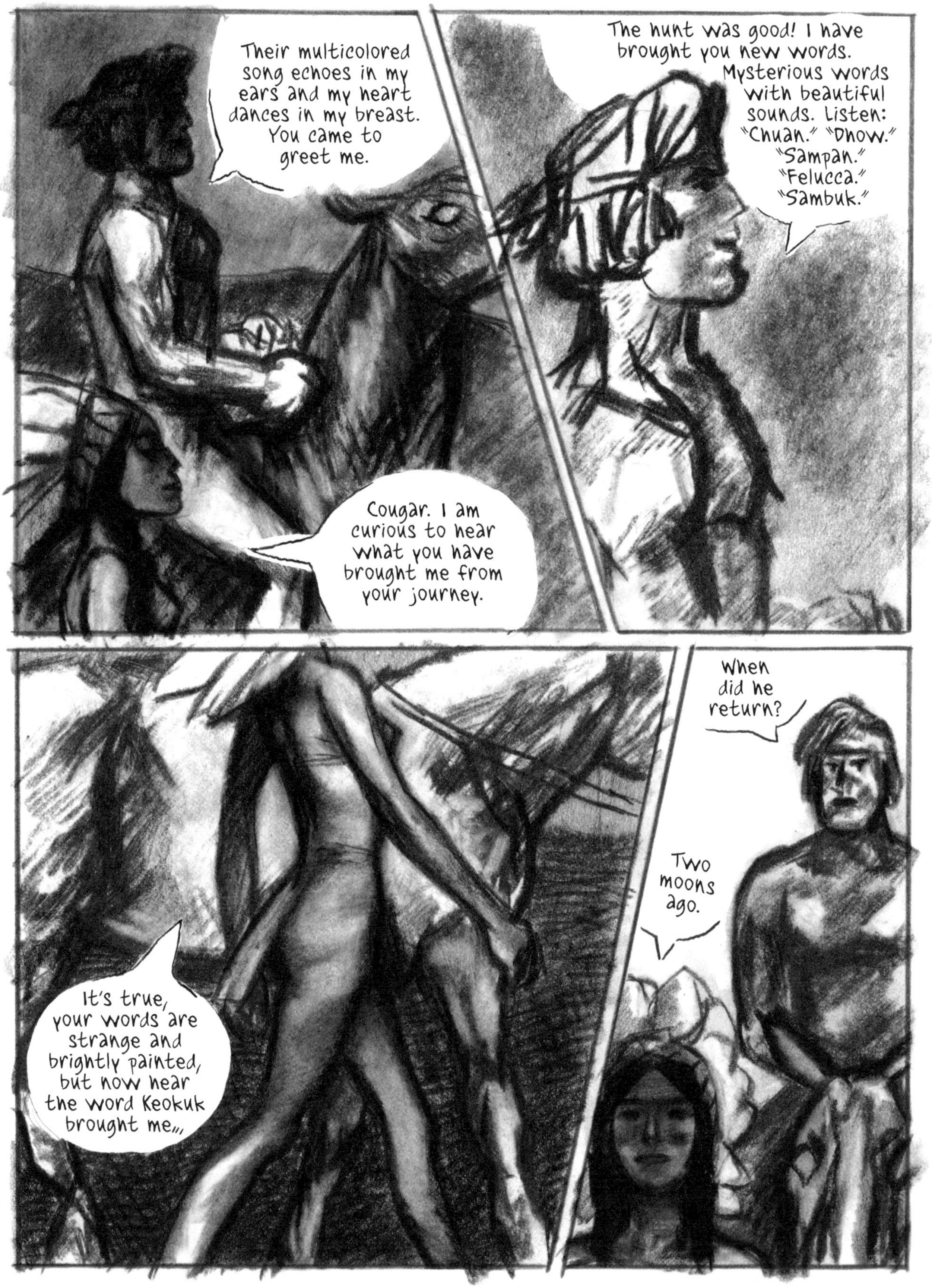
Their multicolored song echoes in my ears and my heart dances in my breast. You came to greet me.
Cougar. I am curious to hear what you have brought me from your journey.
The hunt was good! I have brought you new words. Mysterious words with beautiful sounds. Listen: "Chuan." "Dhow." "Sampan." "Felucca." "Sambuk."
It's true, your words are strange and brightly painted, but now hear the word Keokuk brought me...
When did he return?
Two moons ago.

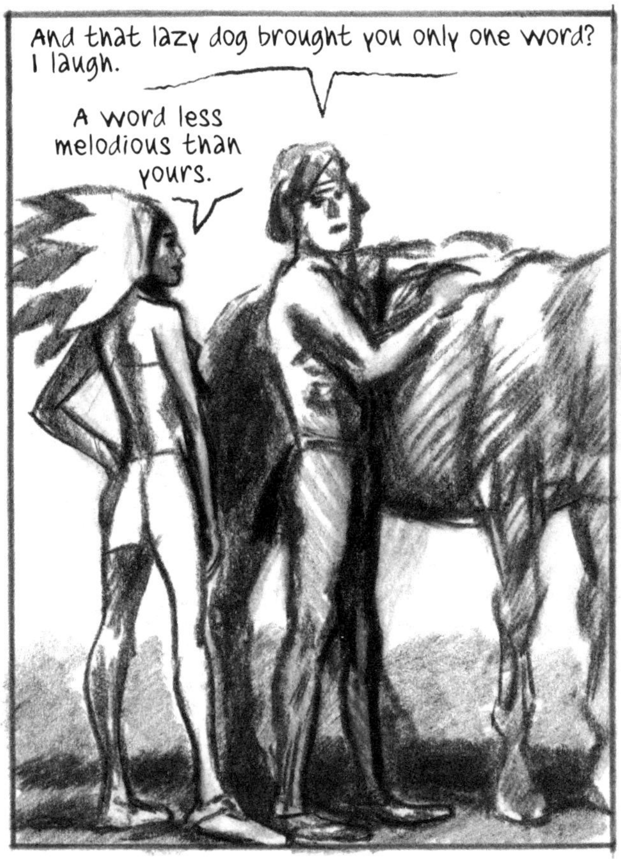
And that lazy dog brought you only one word? I laugh.
A word less melodious than yours.

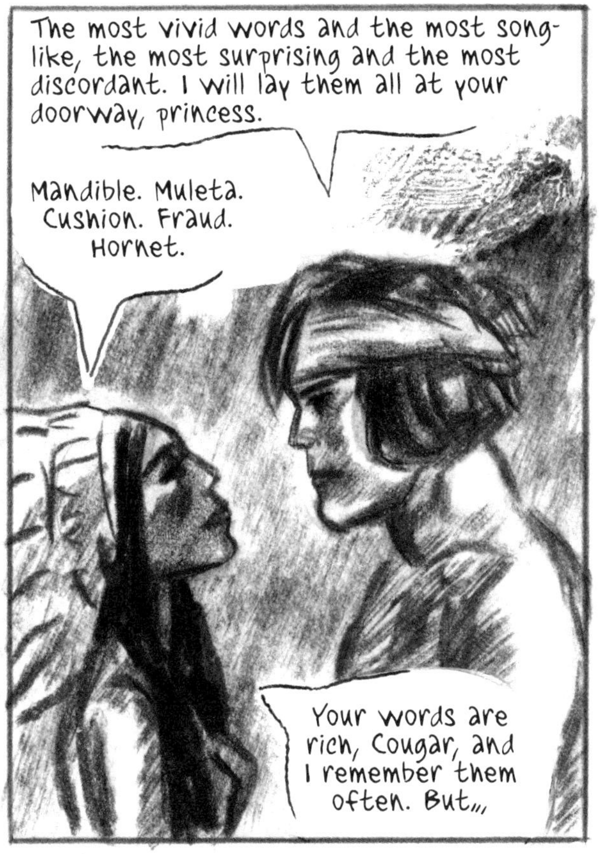
The most vivid words and the most song-like, the most surprising and the most discordant. I will lay them all at your doorway, princess.
Mandible. Muleta. Cushion. Fraud. Hornet.
Your words are rich, Cougar, and I remember them often. But...

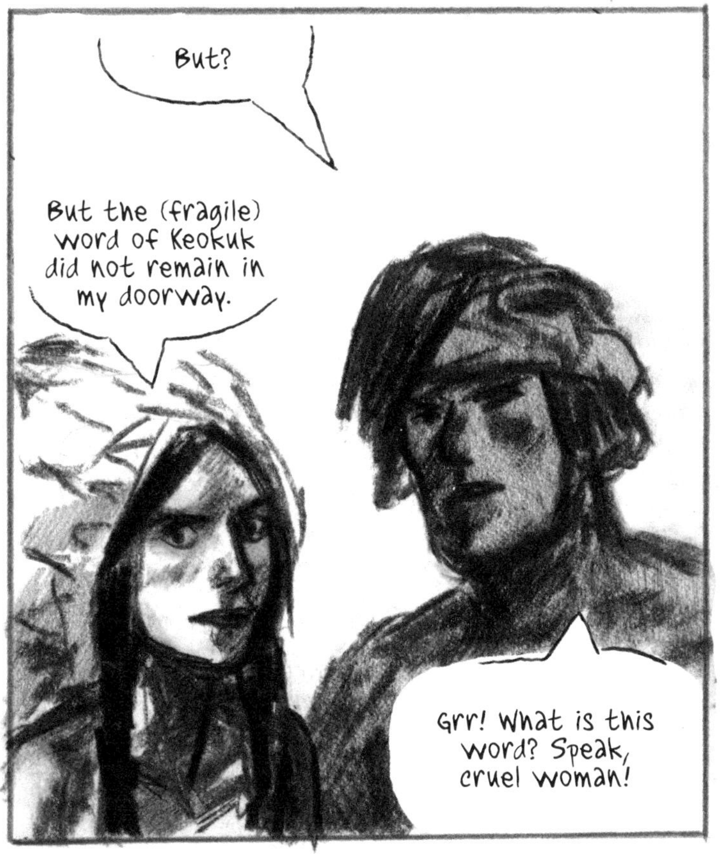
But?
But the (fragile) word of Keokuk did not remain in my doorway.
Grr! What is this word? Speak, cruel woman!

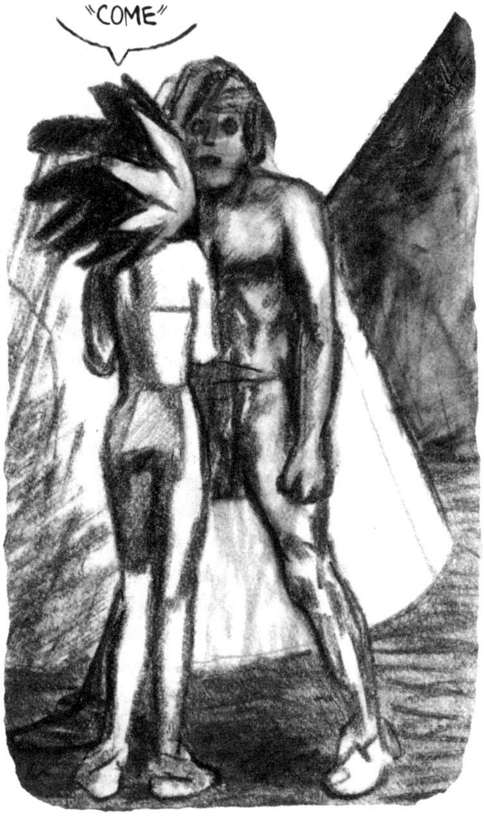
"COME"

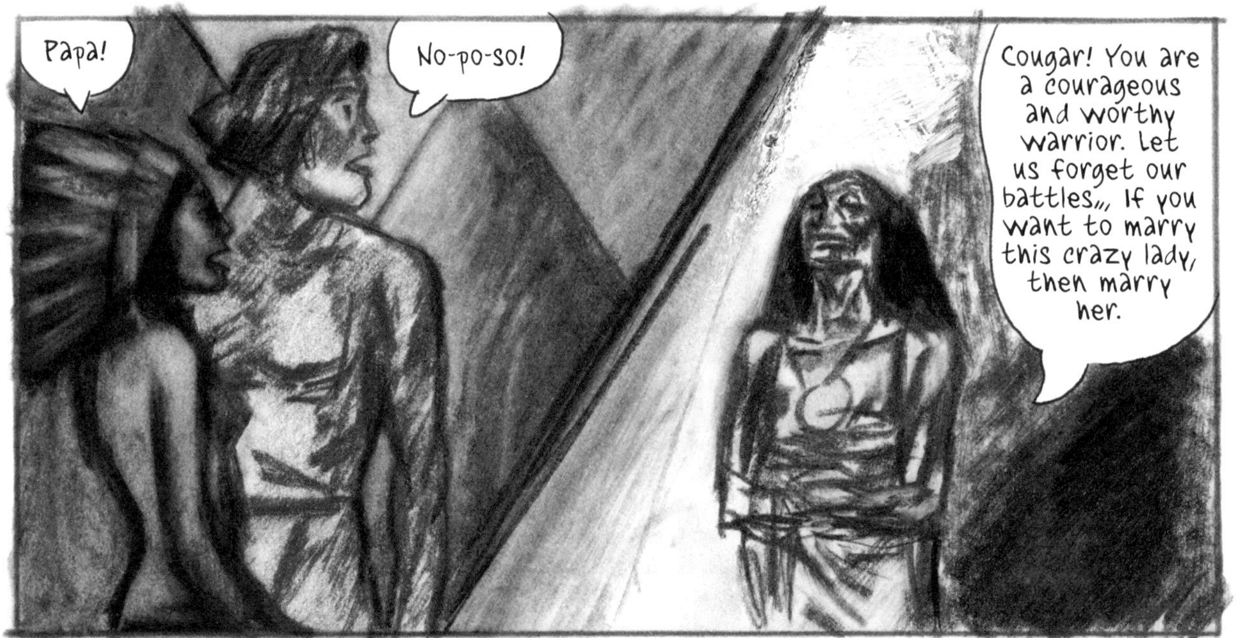
Papa!
No-po-so!
Cougar! You are a courageous and worthy warrior. Let us forget our battles... If you want to marry this crazy lady, then marry her.

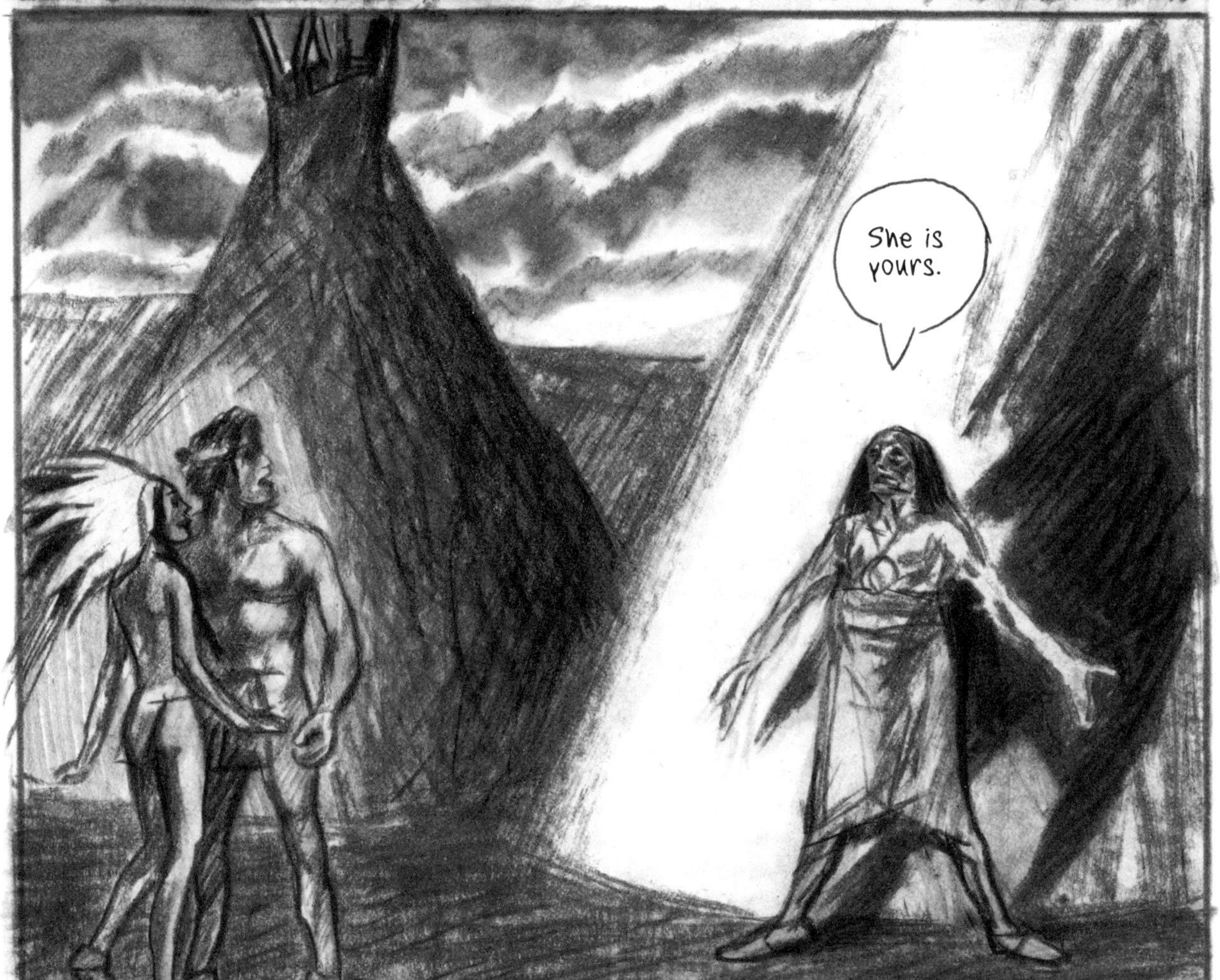
She is yours.

the sound

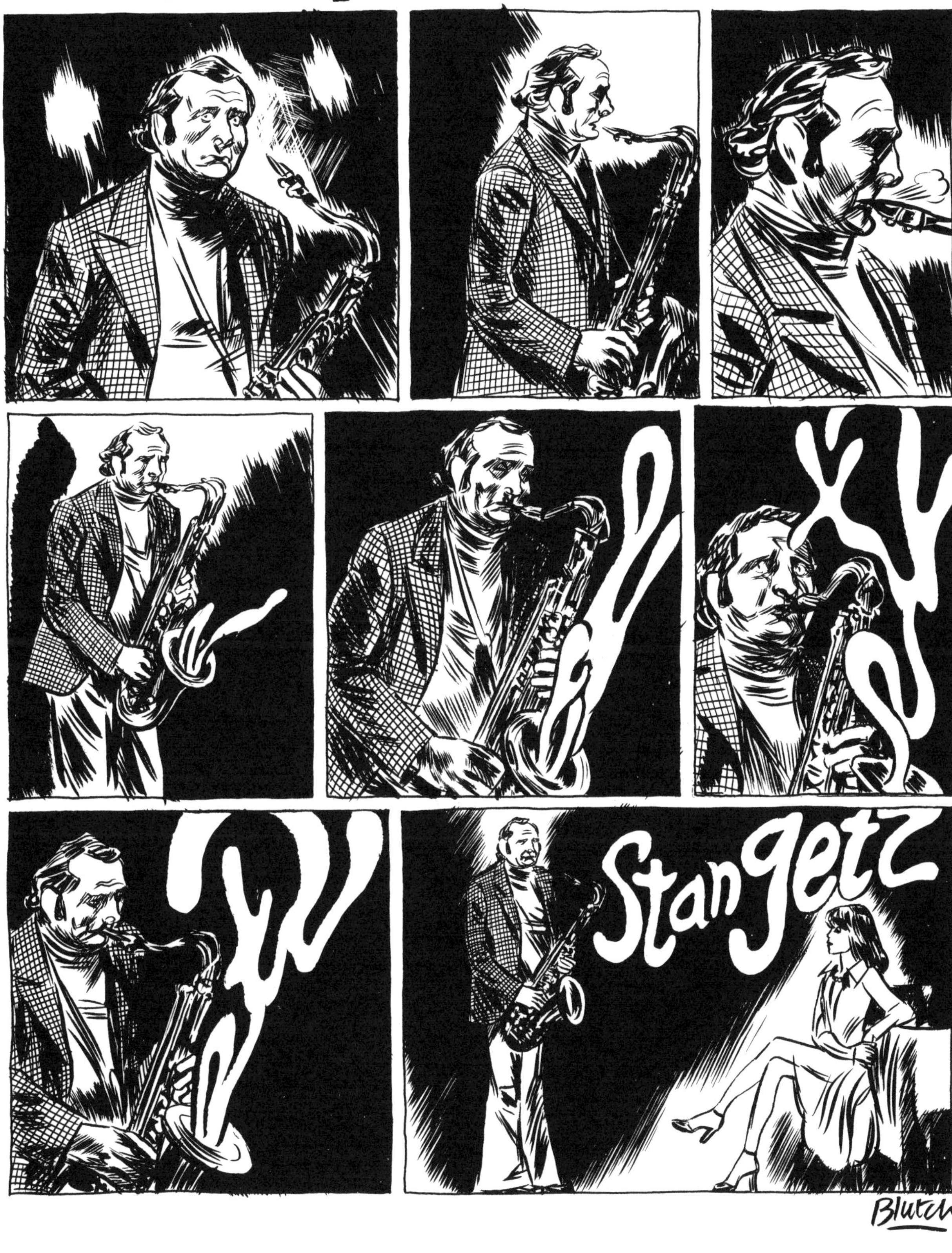
Stan Getz
Blutch

the scene

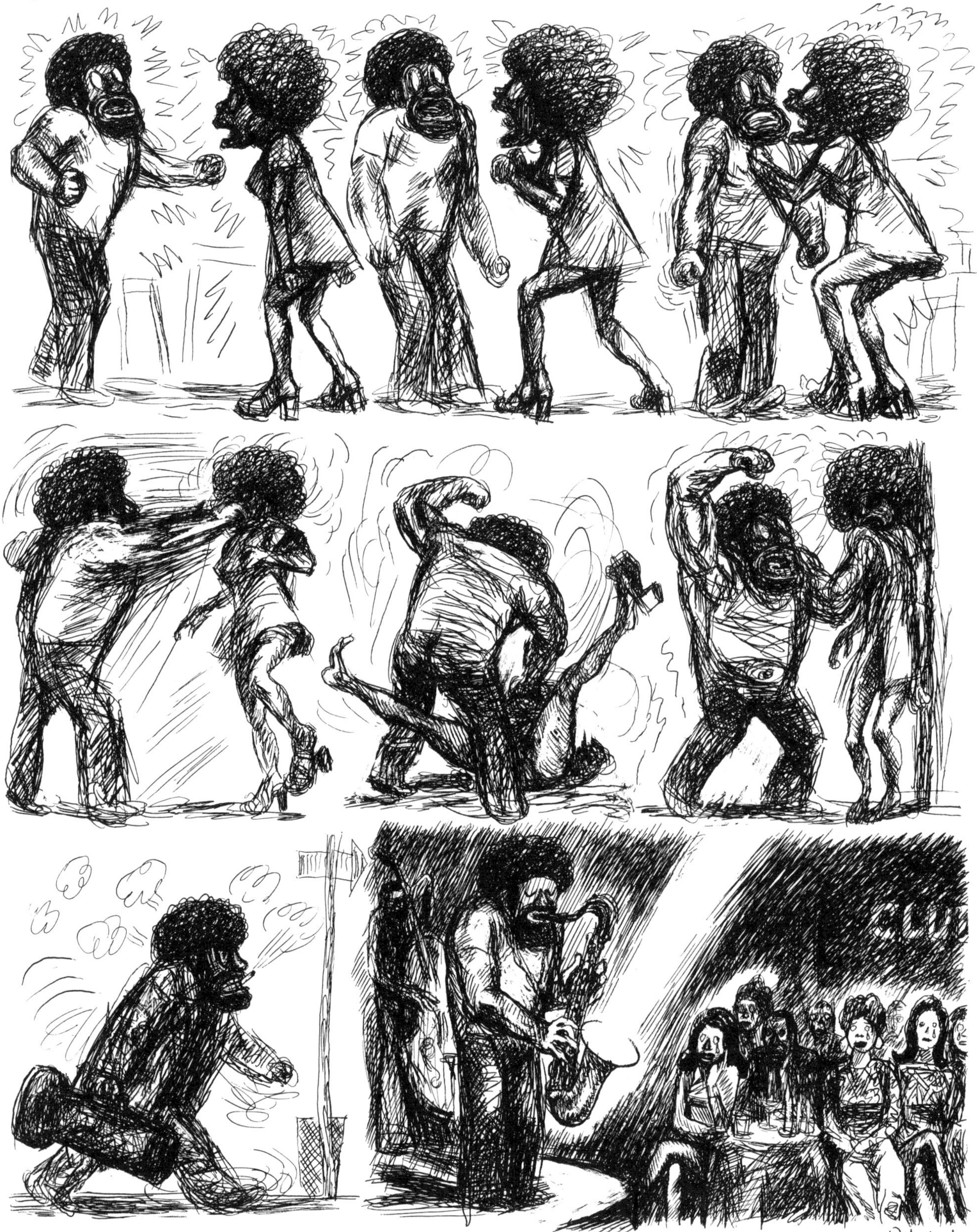

Blutch

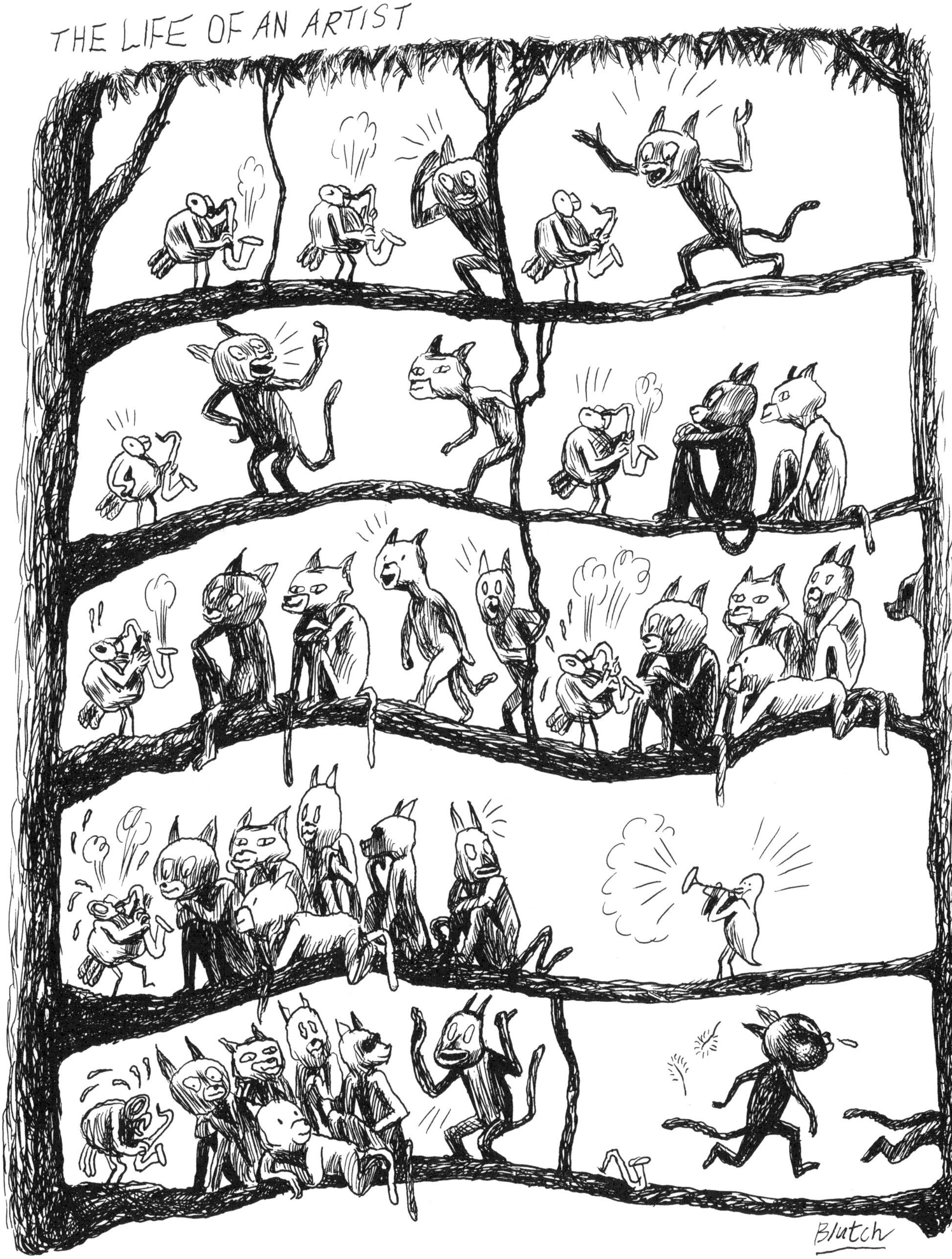
THE LIFE OF AN ARTIST
Blutch

wayne live

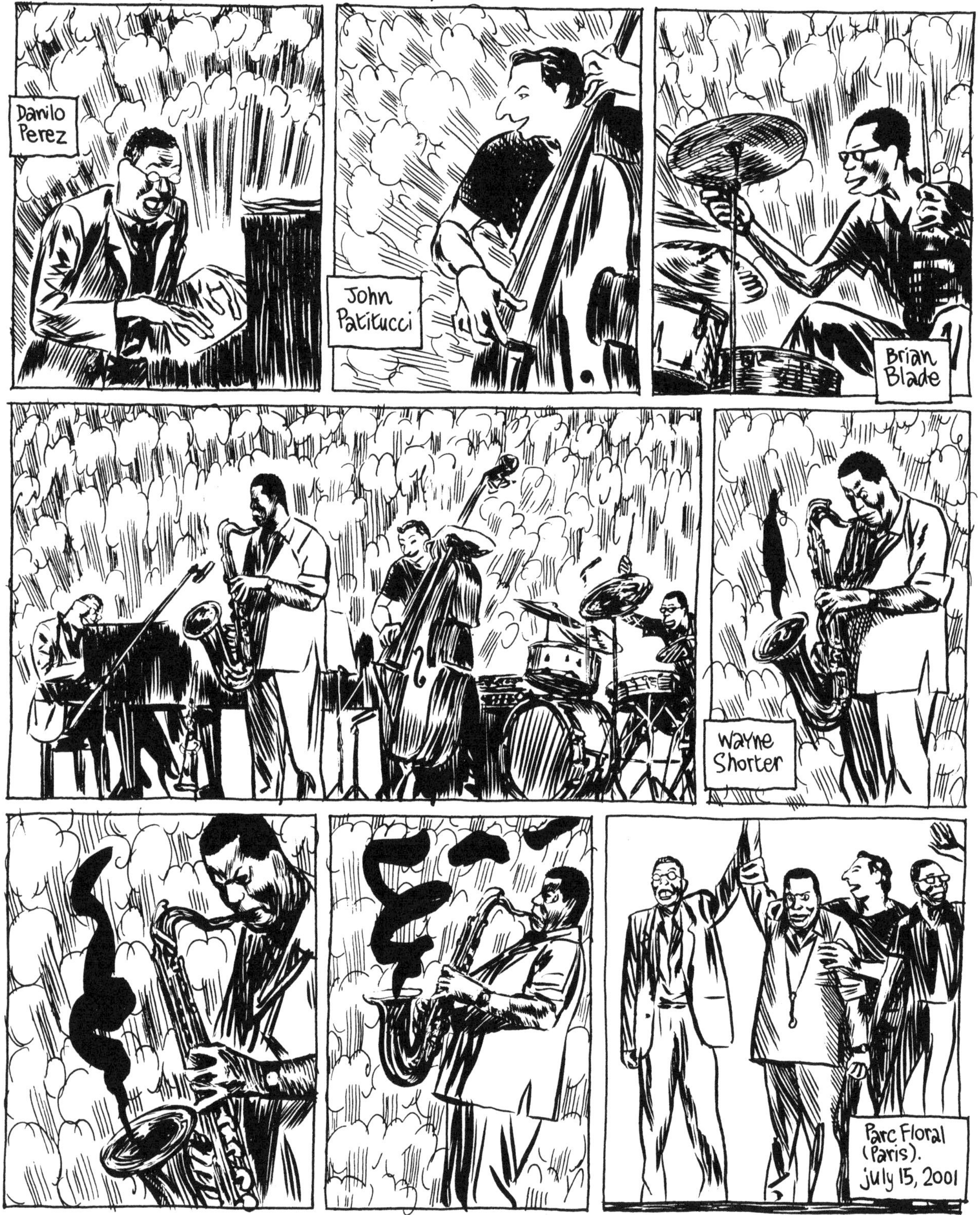
Danilo Perez
John Patitucci
Brian Blade
Wayne Shorter
Parc Floral (Paris). july 15, 2001
Blutch

the muse

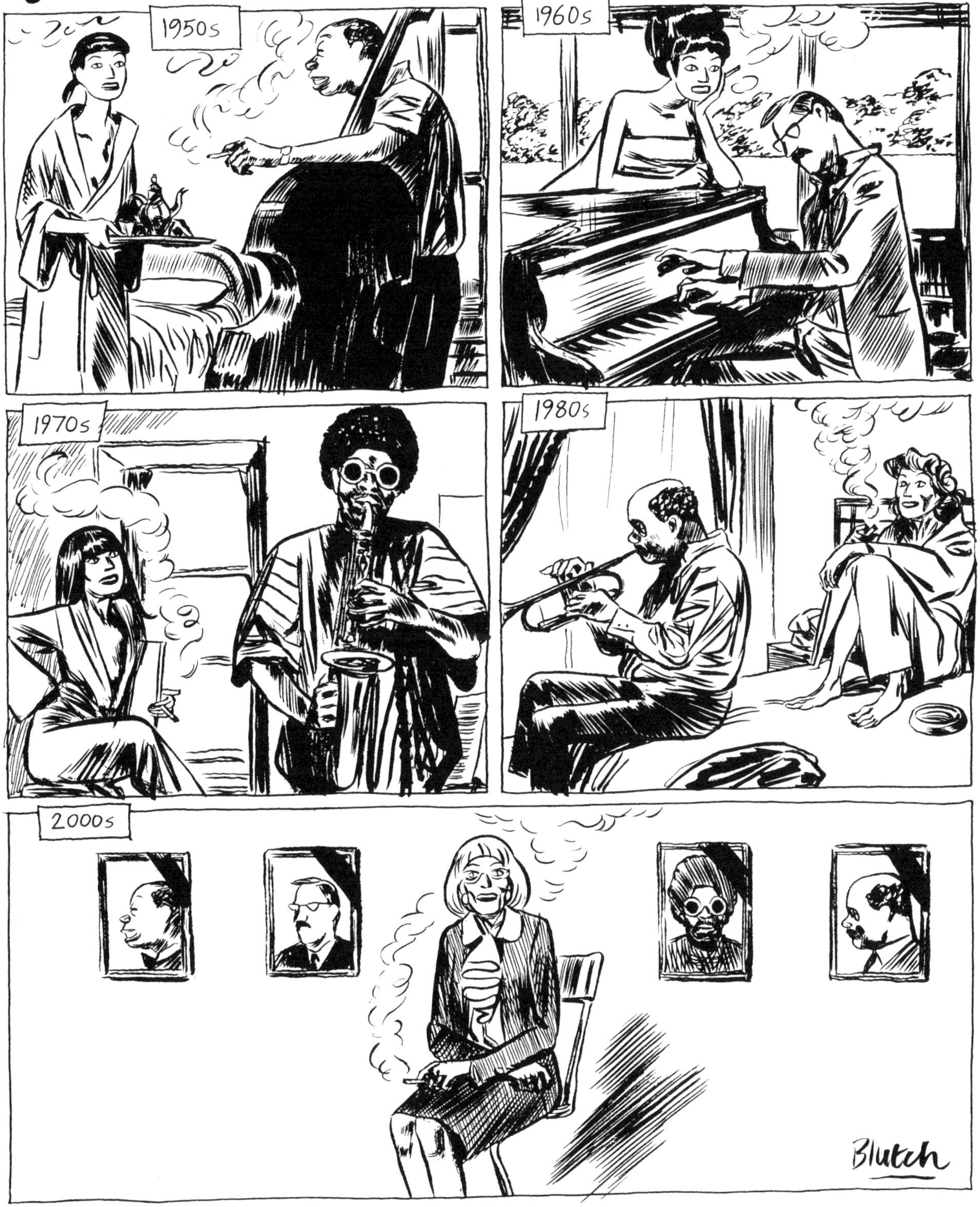
1950s
1960s
1970s
1980s
2000s
Blutch

five solos (a selection)

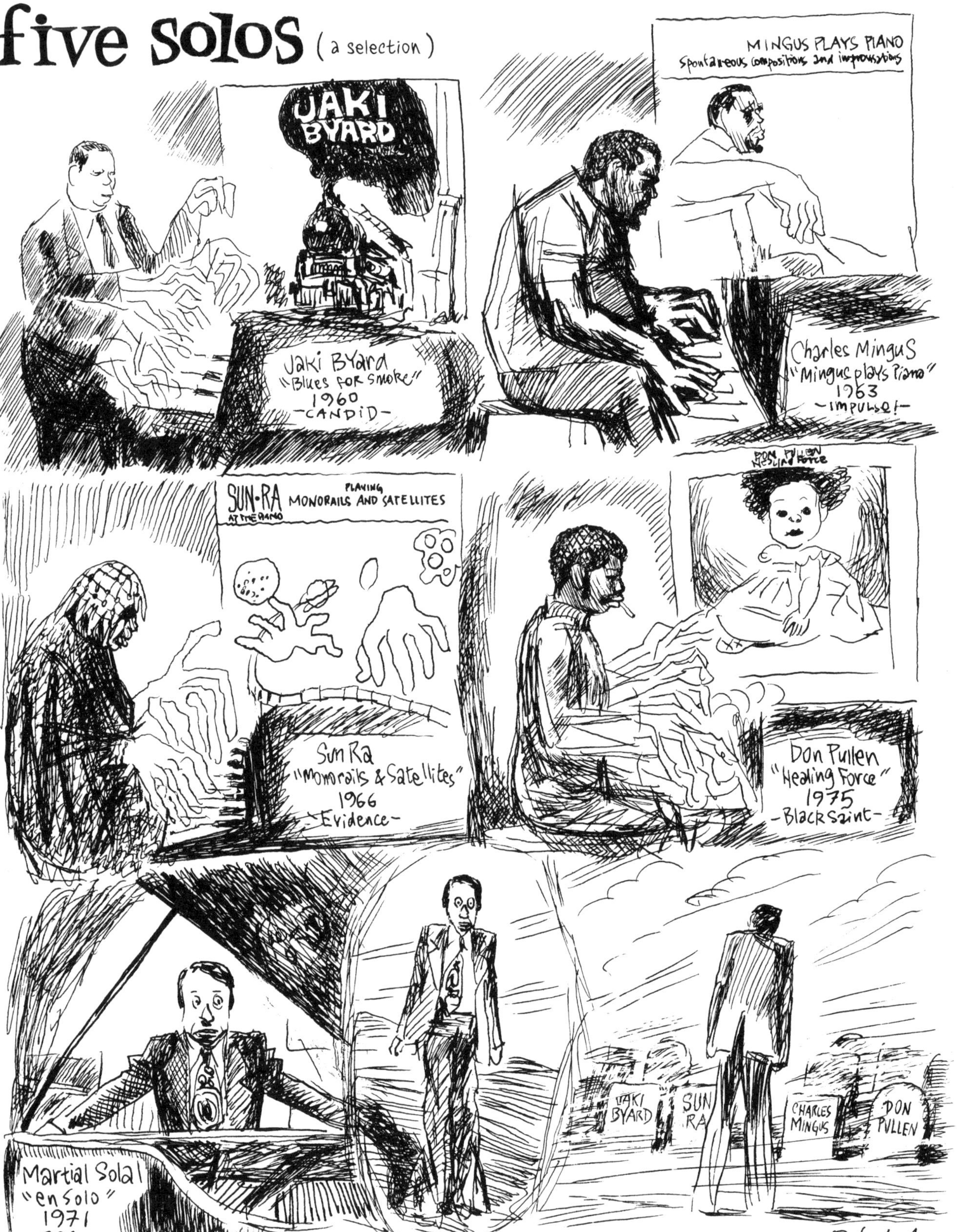
JAKI BYARD
Jaki Byard
"Blues for Smoke"
1960
-CANDID-
MINGUS PLAYS PIANO
Spontaneous compositions and improvisations
Charles Mingus
"Mingus plays Piano"
1963
-IMPULSE!-
SUN-RA AT THE PIANO
PLAYING MONORAILS AND SATELLITES
Sun Ra
"Monorails & Satellites"
1966
-Evidence-
DON PULLEN HEALING FORCE
Don Pullen
"Healing Force"
1975
-Black Saint-
Martial Solal
"en Solo"
1971
- RCA -
JAKI BYARD
SUN RA
CHARLES MINGUS
DON PULLEN
Blutch

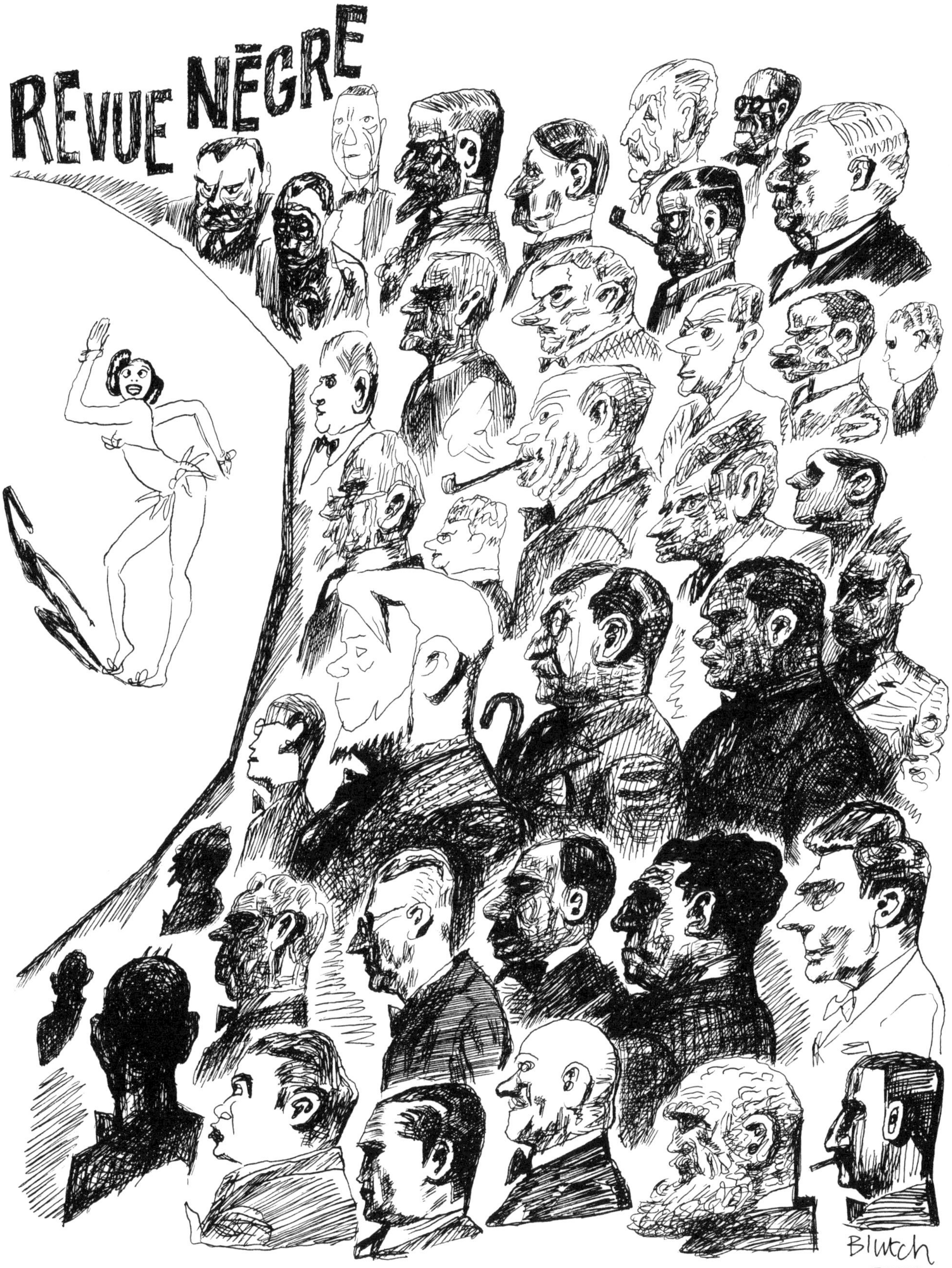
REVUE NÈGRE
Blutch

creole orchestra

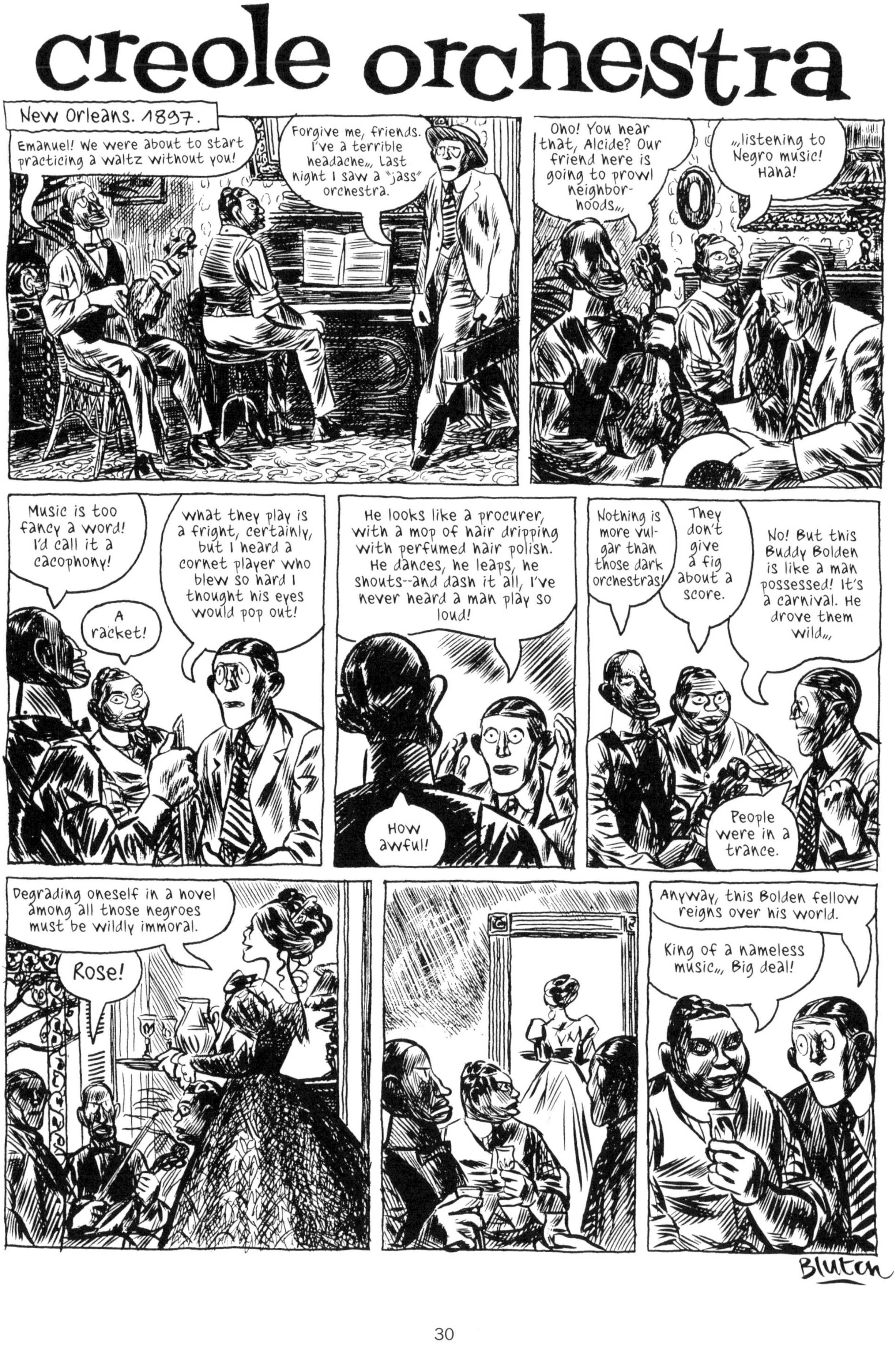
New Orleans. 1897.
Emanuel! We were about to start practicing a waltz without you!
Forgive me, friends. I've a terrible headache... Last night I saw a "jass" orchestra.
Oho! You hear that, Alcide? Our friend here is going to prowl neighbor-hoods...
...listening to Negro music! Haha!
Music is too fancy a word! I'd call it a cacophony!
A racket!
What they play is a fright, certainly, but I heard a cornet player who blew so hard I thought his eyes would pop out!
He looks like a procurer, with a mop of hair dripping with perfumed hair polish. He dances, he leaps, he shouts--and dash it all, I've never heard a man play so loud!
How awful!
Nothing is more vul-gar than those dark orchestras!
They don't give a fig about a score.
No! But this Buddy Bolden is like a man possessed! It's a carnival. He drove them wild...
People were in a trance.
Degrading oneself in a hovel among all those negroes must be wildly immoral.
Rose!
Anyway, this Bolden fellow reigns over his world.
King of a nameless music... Big deal!
Bluten

ode to Buddy Bolden, musician.

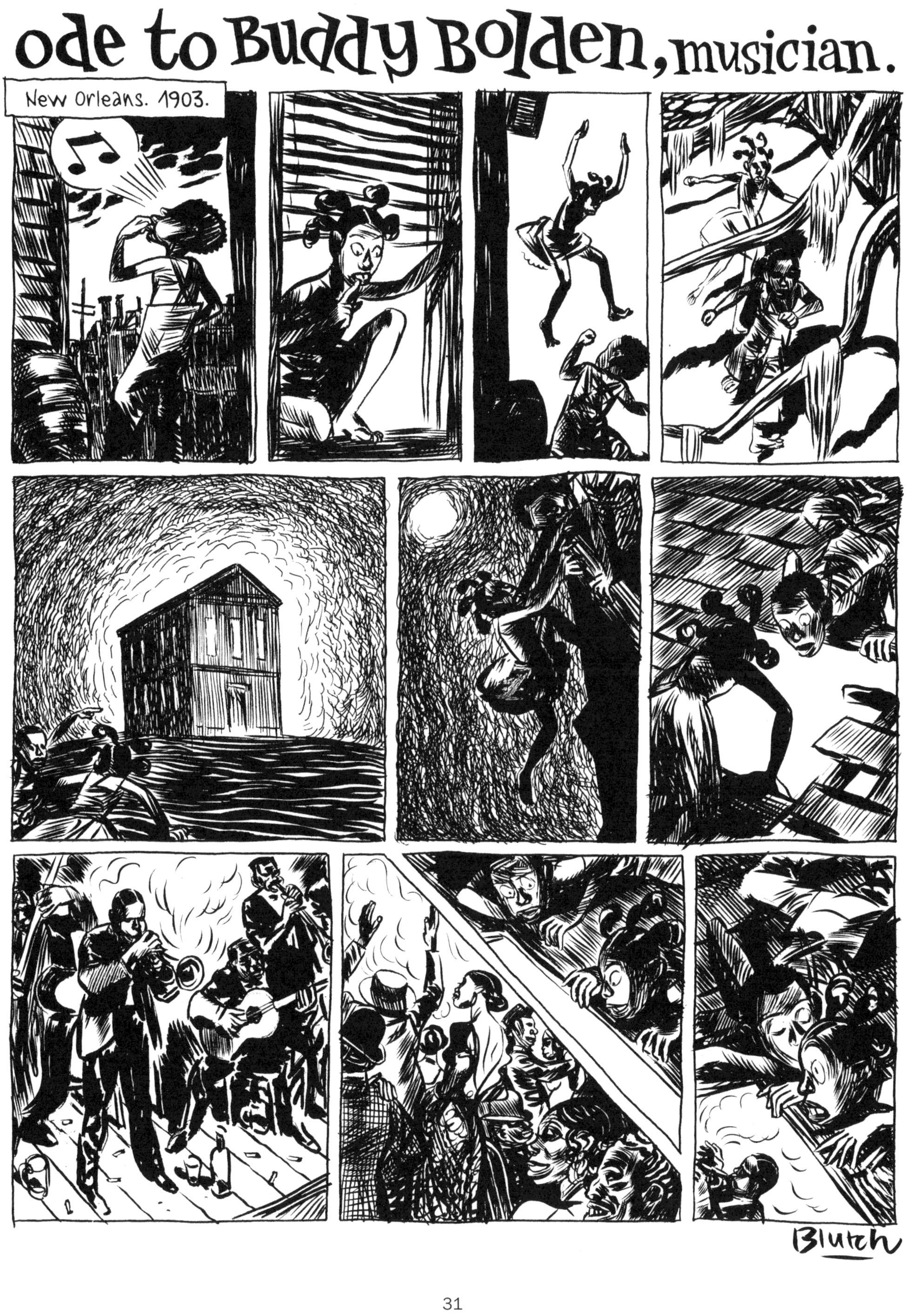
New Orleans. 1903.
♫
Blutch

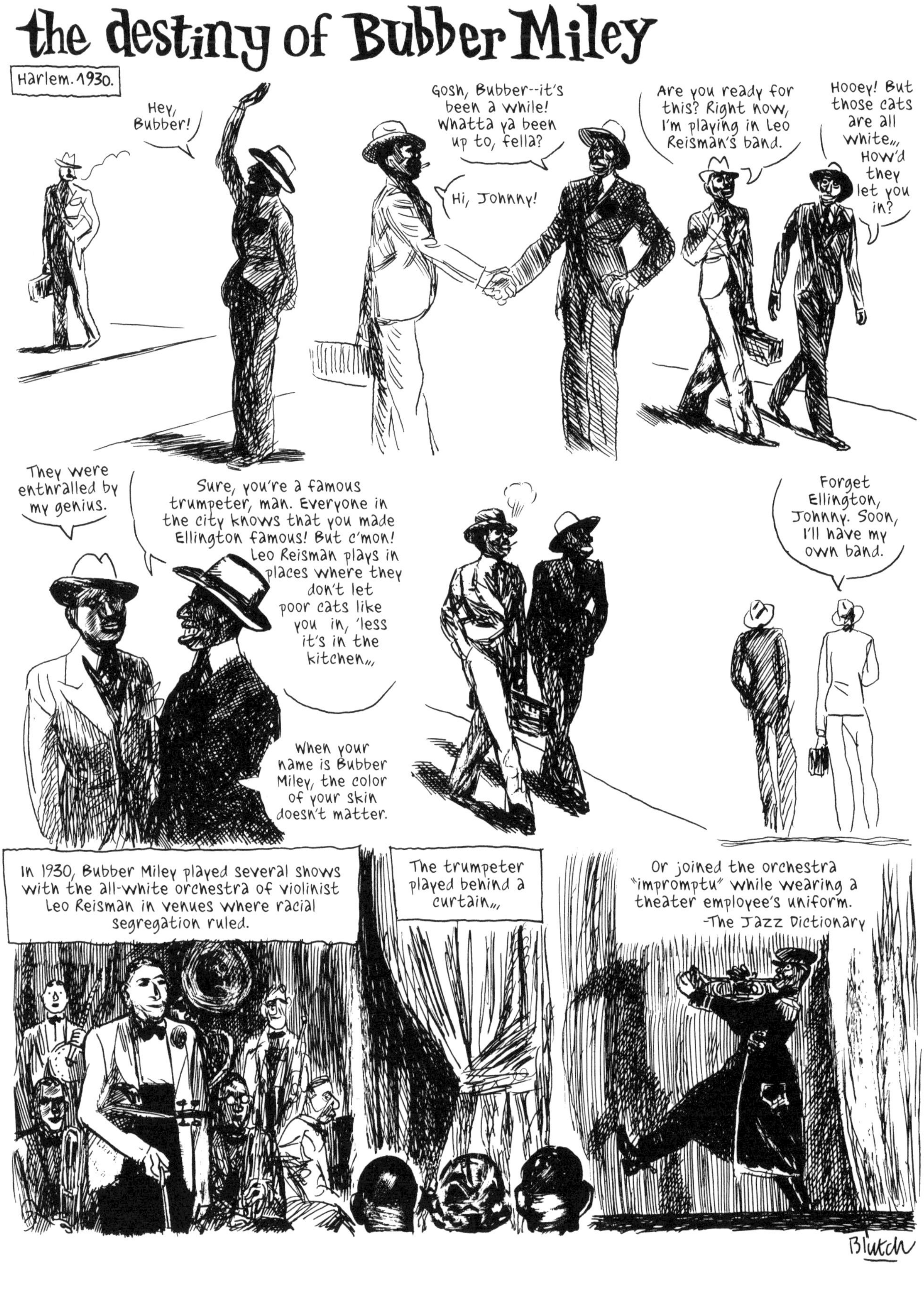
the destiny of Bubber Miley
Harlem. 1930.
Hey, Bubber!
Gosh, Bubber--it's been a while! Whatta ya been up to, fella?
Hi, Johnny!
Are you ready for this? Right now, I'm playing in Leo Reisman's band.
Hooey! But those cats are all white... How'd they let you in?
They were enthralled by my genius.
Sure, you're a famous trumpeter, man. Everyone in the city knows that you made Ellington famous! But c'mon! Leo Reisman plays in places where they don't let poor cats like you in, 'less it's in the kitchen...
When your name is Bubber Miley, the color of your skin doesn't matter.
Forget Ellington, Johnny. Soon, I'll have my own band.
In 1930, Bubber Miley played several shows with the all-white orchestra of violinist Leo Reisman in venues where racial segregation ruled.
The trumpeter played behind a curtain...
Or joined the orchestra "impromptu" while wearing a theater employee's uniform.
-The Jazz Dictionary
Blutch

My Parisian life

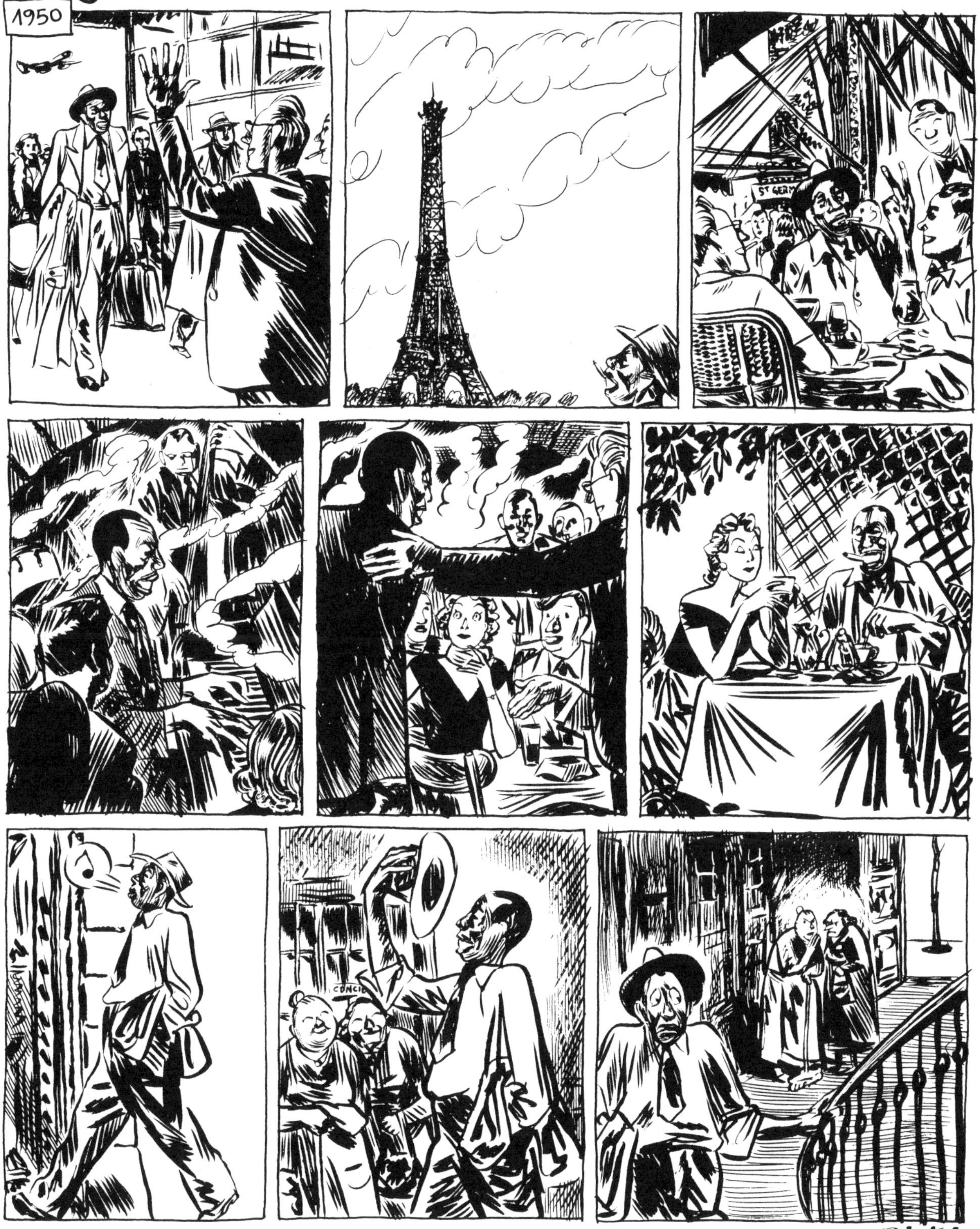
1950
Blutch

Study
ON the PREJUDICE OF CLASSIC COMICS toward JAZZ

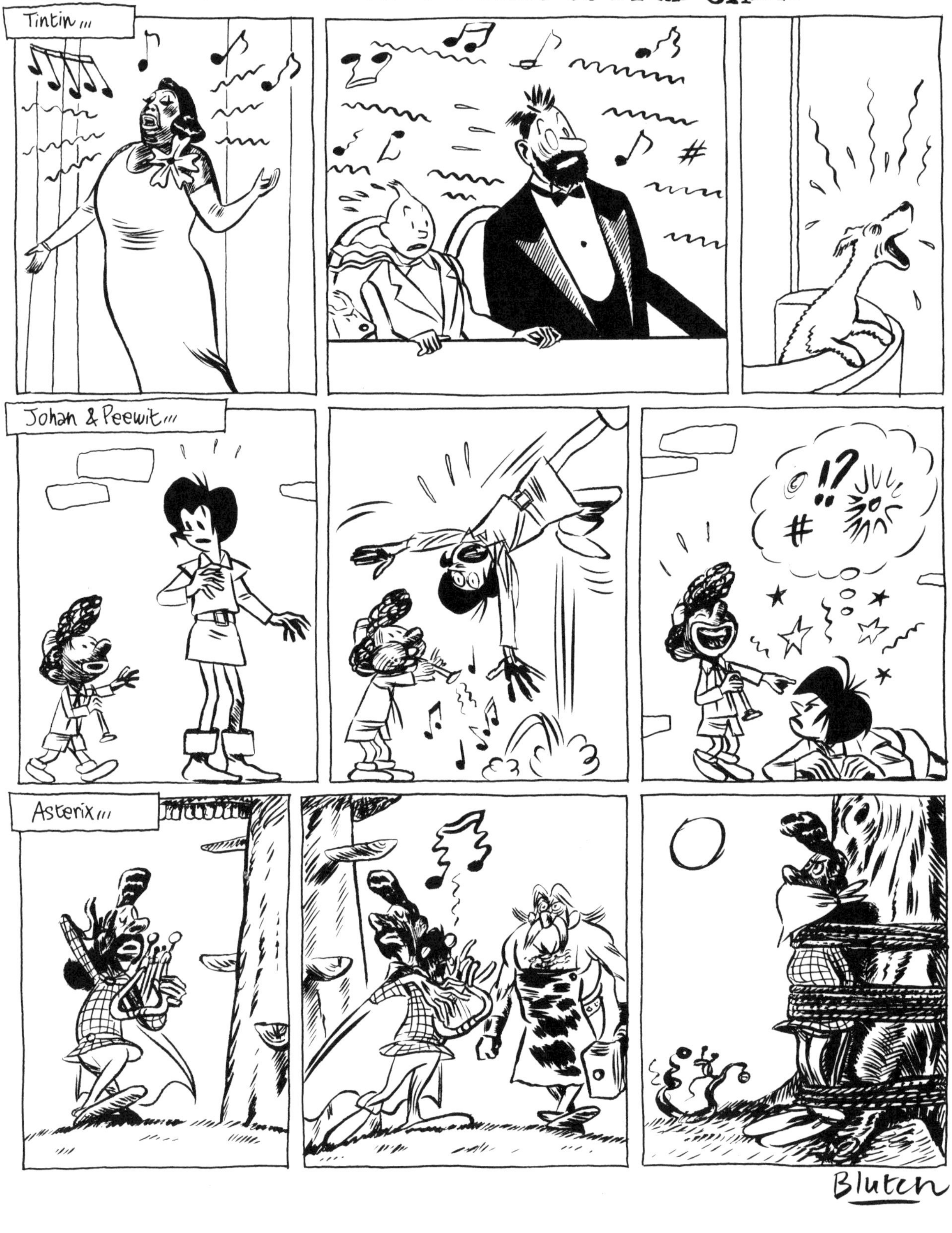

Tintin...
Johan & Peewit...
Asterix...
Blutch

Pop stars at home

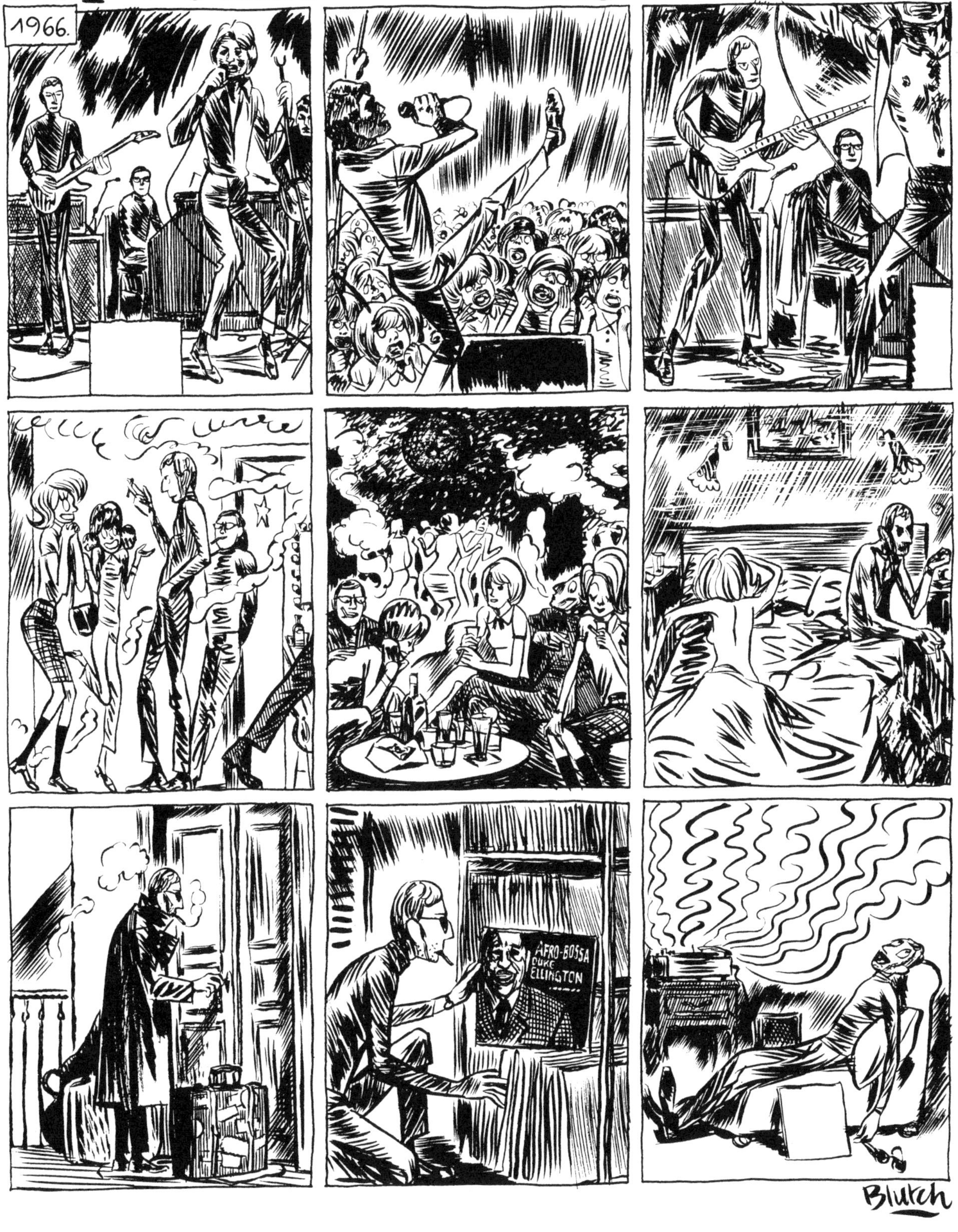
1966.
AFRO-BOSSA
DUKE ELLINGTON
Blutch

neighbors

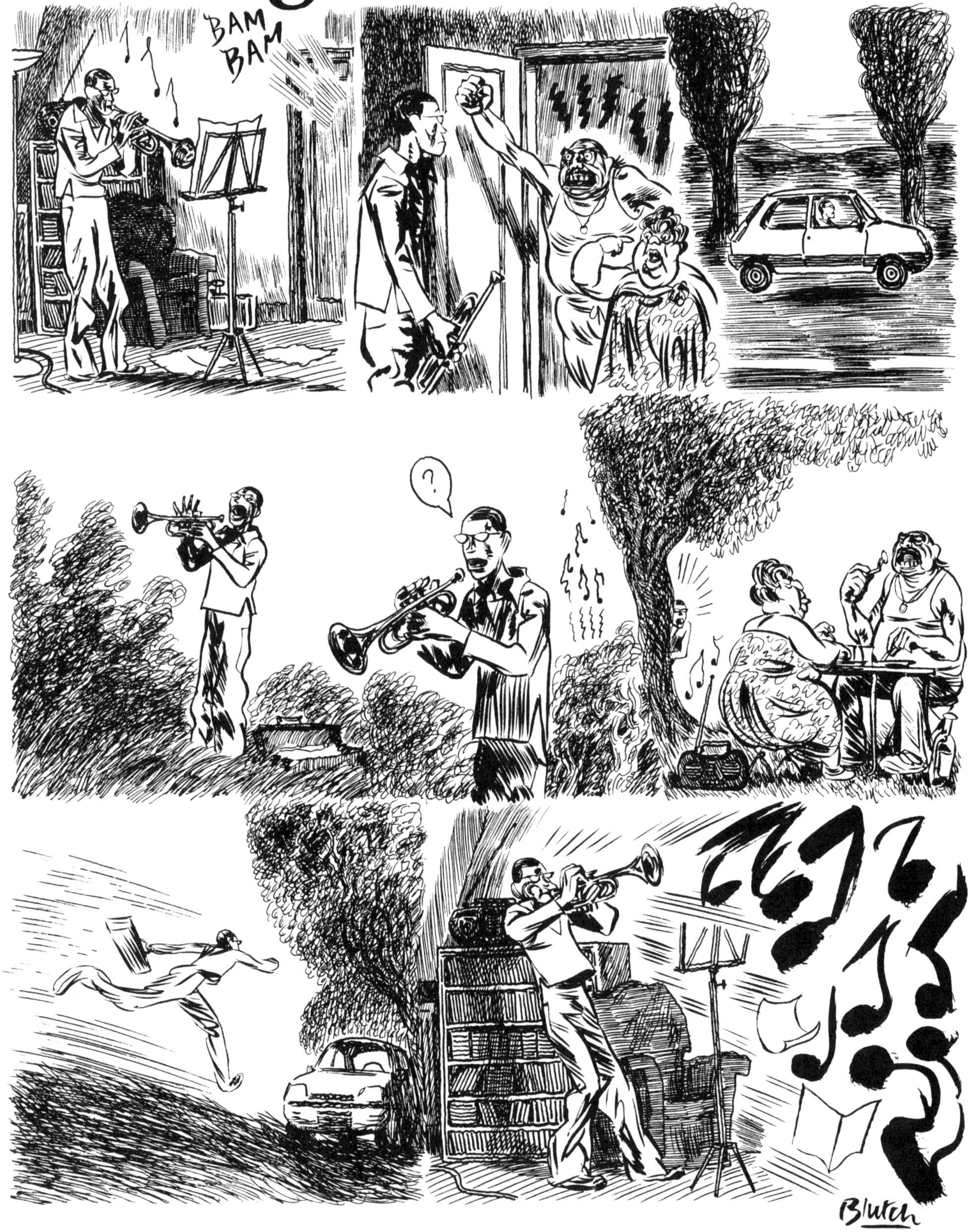
BAM
BAM
?
Blutch

SONNY SHARROCK

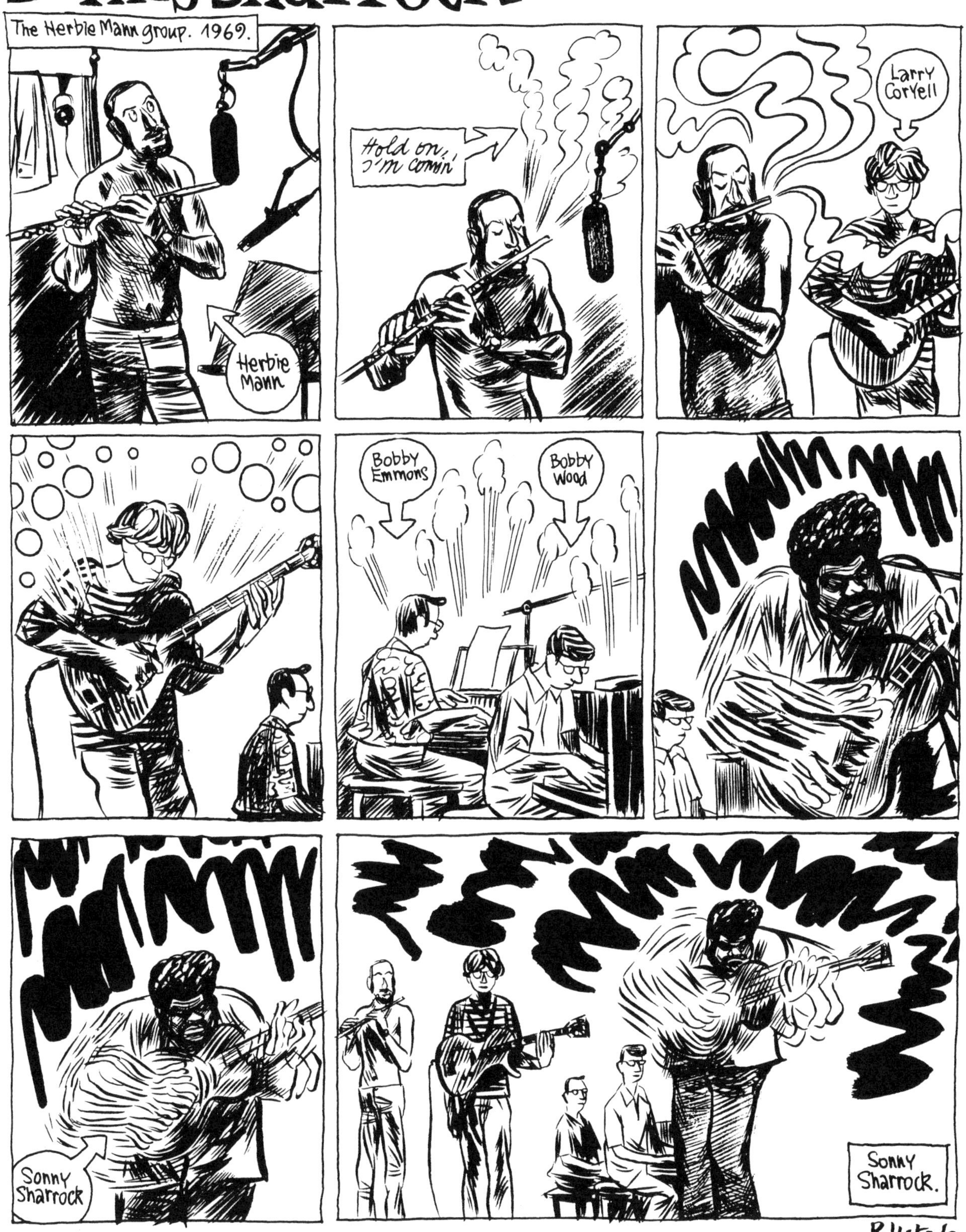

The Herbie Mann group. 1969.
Herbie Mann
Hold on, I'm comin'
Larry Coryell
Bobby Emmons
Bobby Wood
Sonny Sharrock
Sonny Sharrock.

Blutch

Summer Breeze

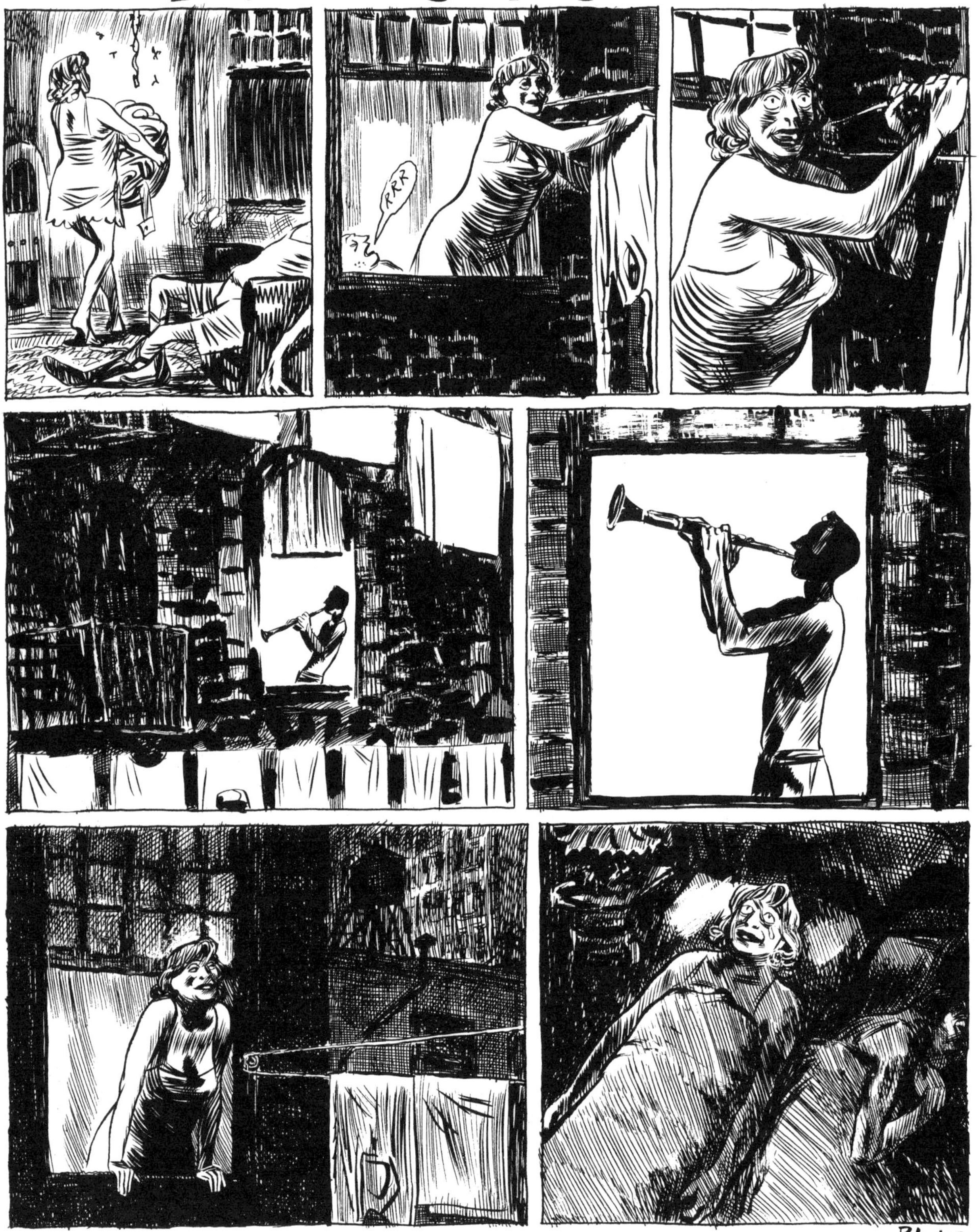
RRR

Blutch

Summer Night (Fire Escape)

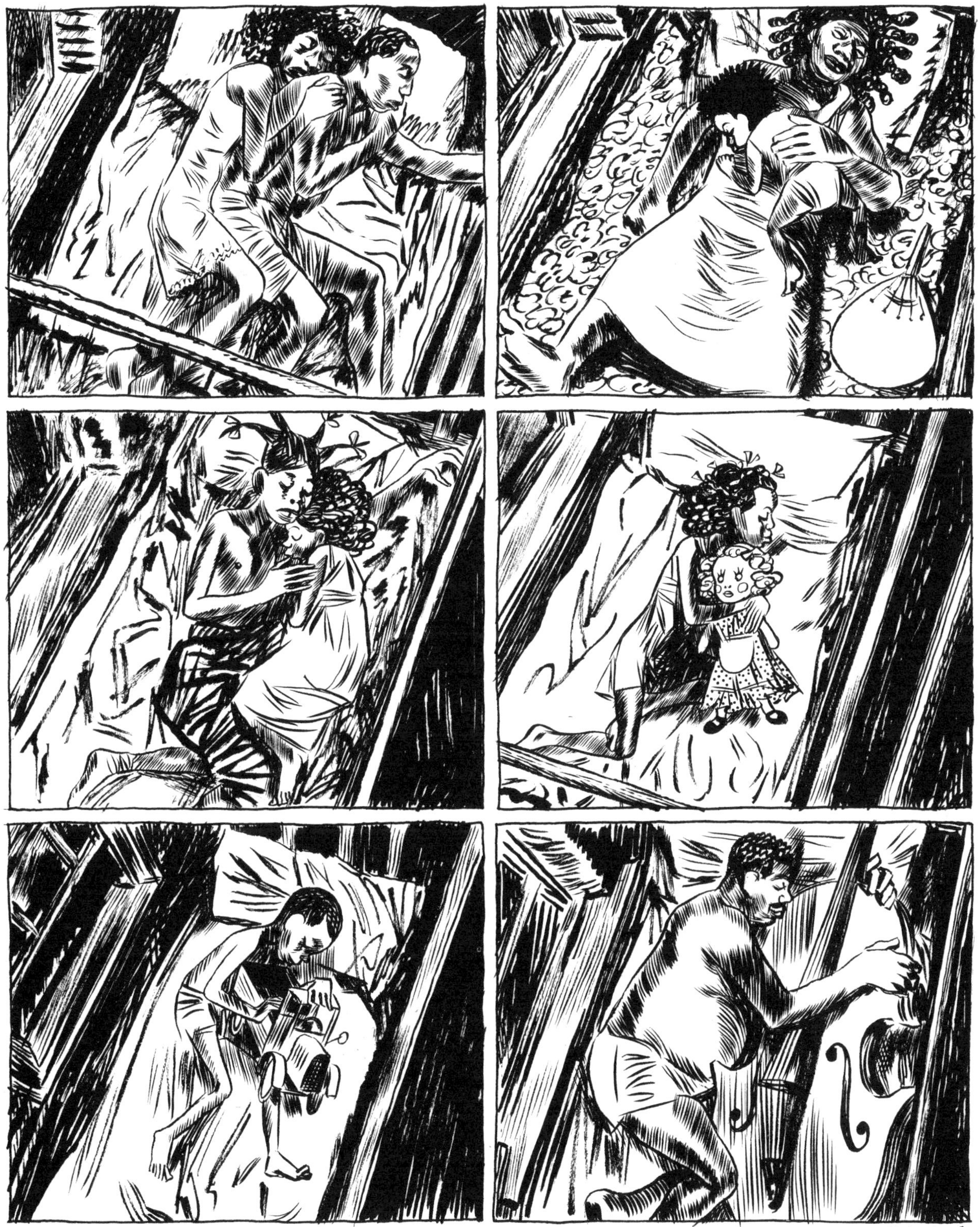

Blutch

jazz in the middle ages

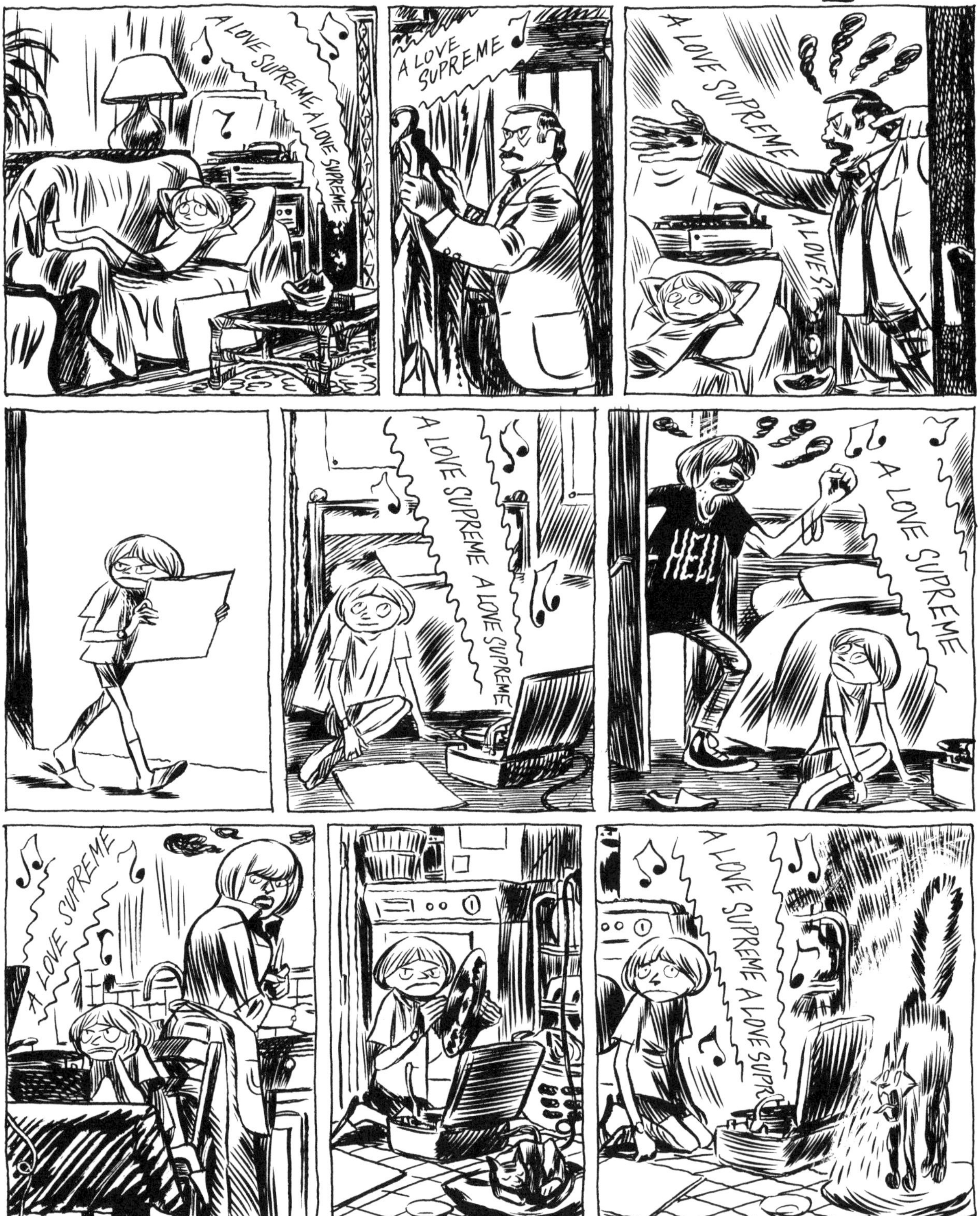
A LOVE SUPREME A LOVE SUPREME
A LOVE SUPREME
A LOVE SUPREME A LOVE S
A LOVE SUPREME A LOVE SUPREME A LOVE SUPREME
HELL
A LOVE SUPREME
A LOVE SUPREME
A LOVE SUPREME A LOVE SUPREME A LOVE SUPRE

Blutch

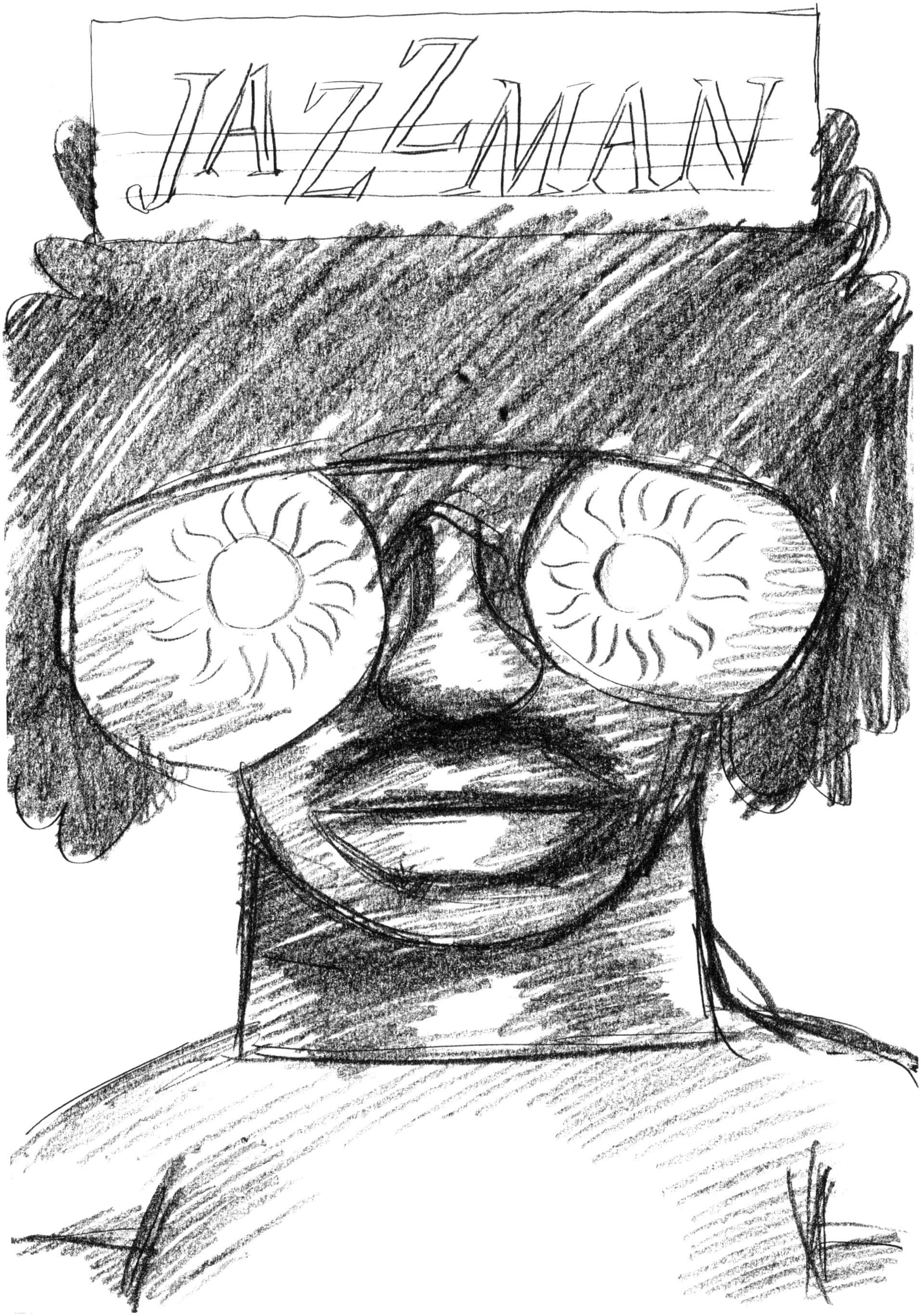
JAZZMAN

Practice

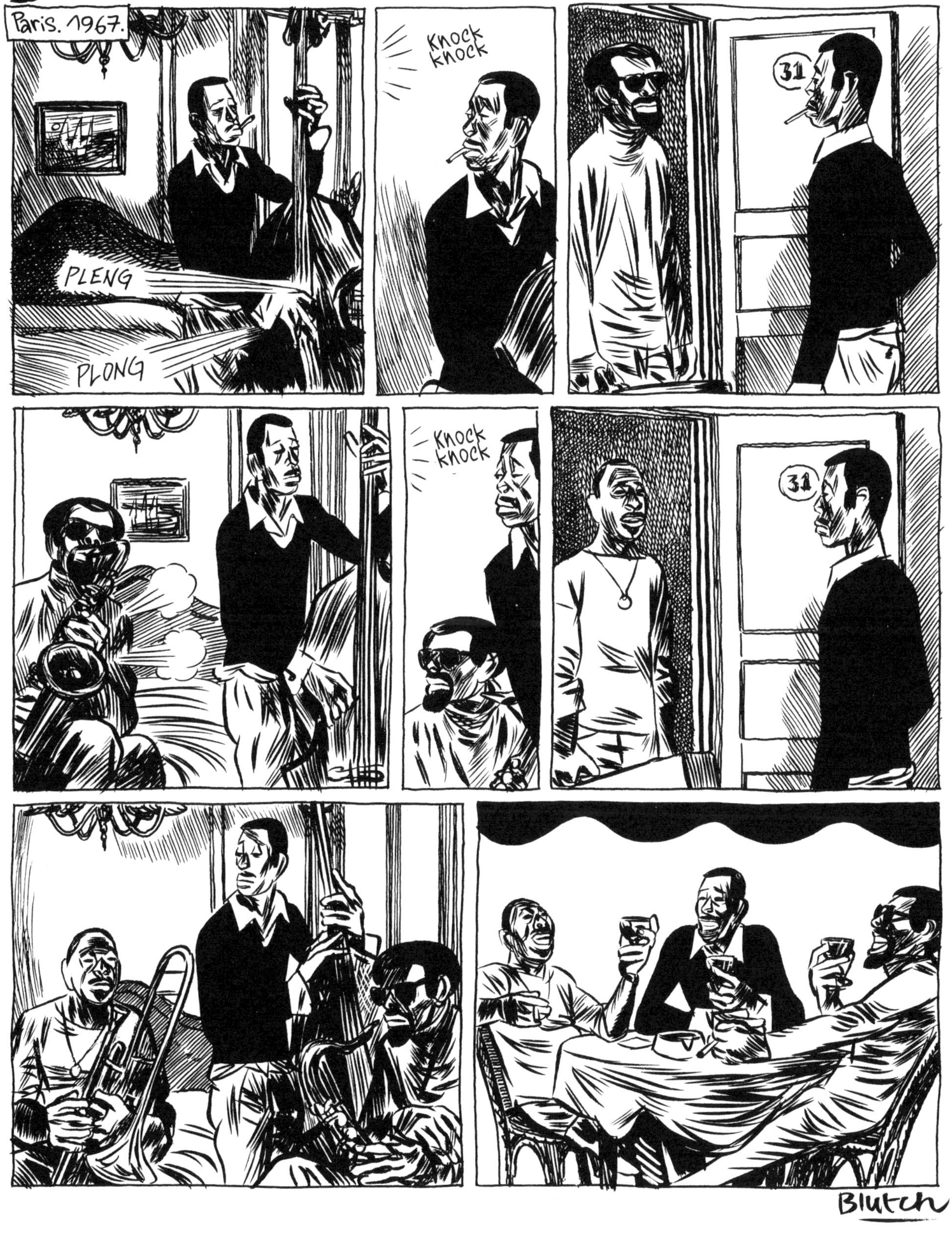

Paris. 1967.
PLENG
PLONG
Knock knock
31
Knock knock
31
Blutch

the audition

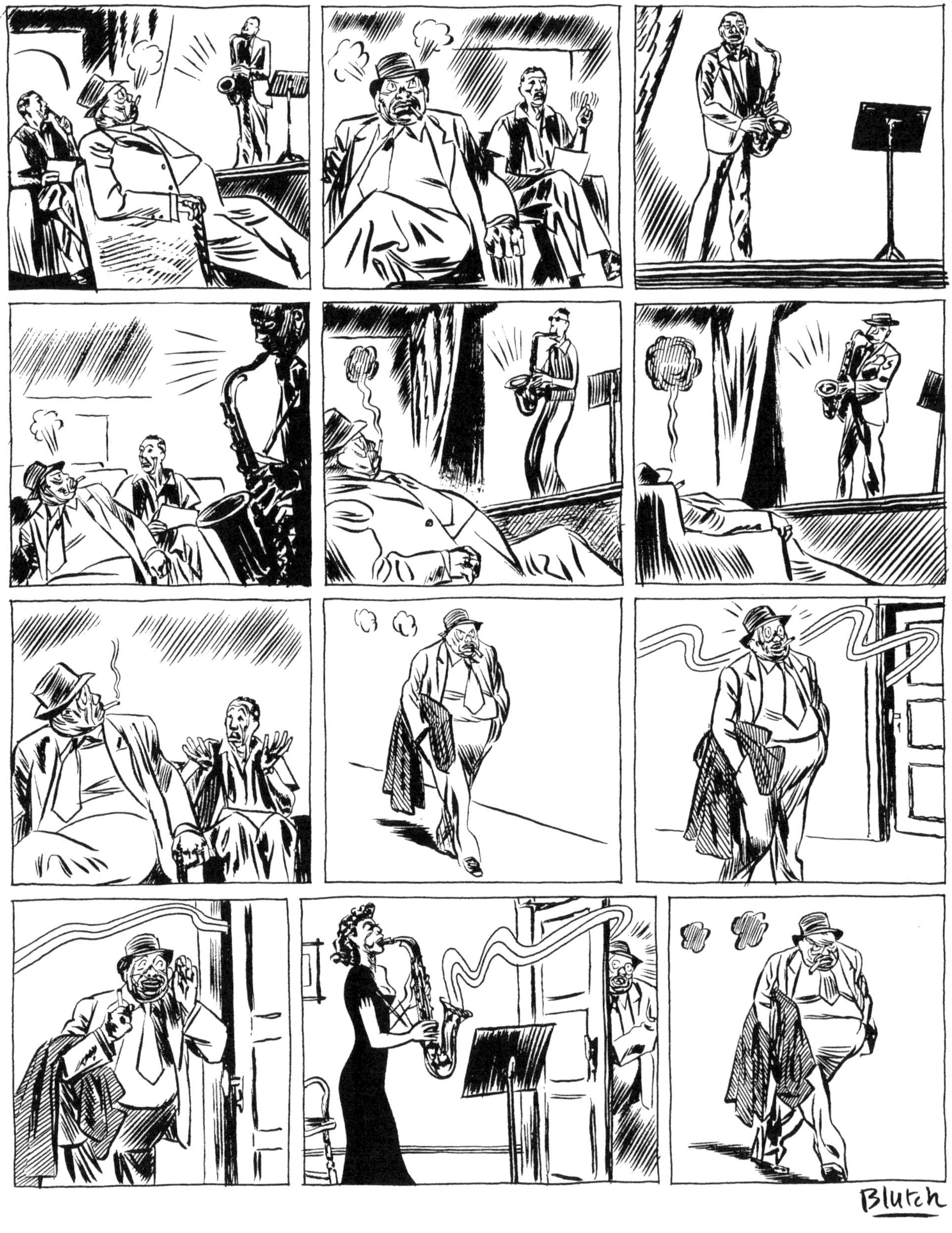
Blutch

traffic jam

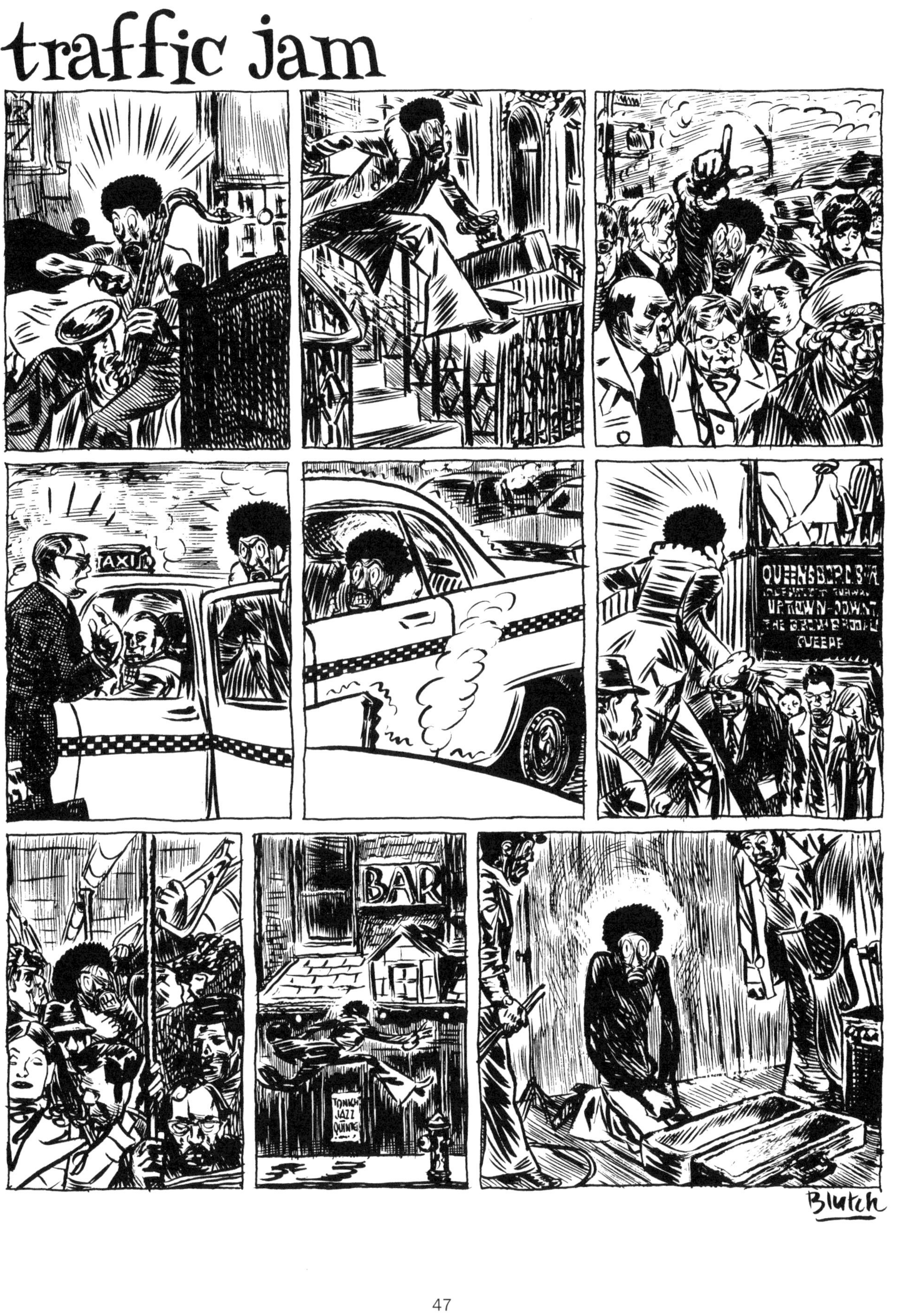
TAXI
BAR
JAZZ

Blutch

summit

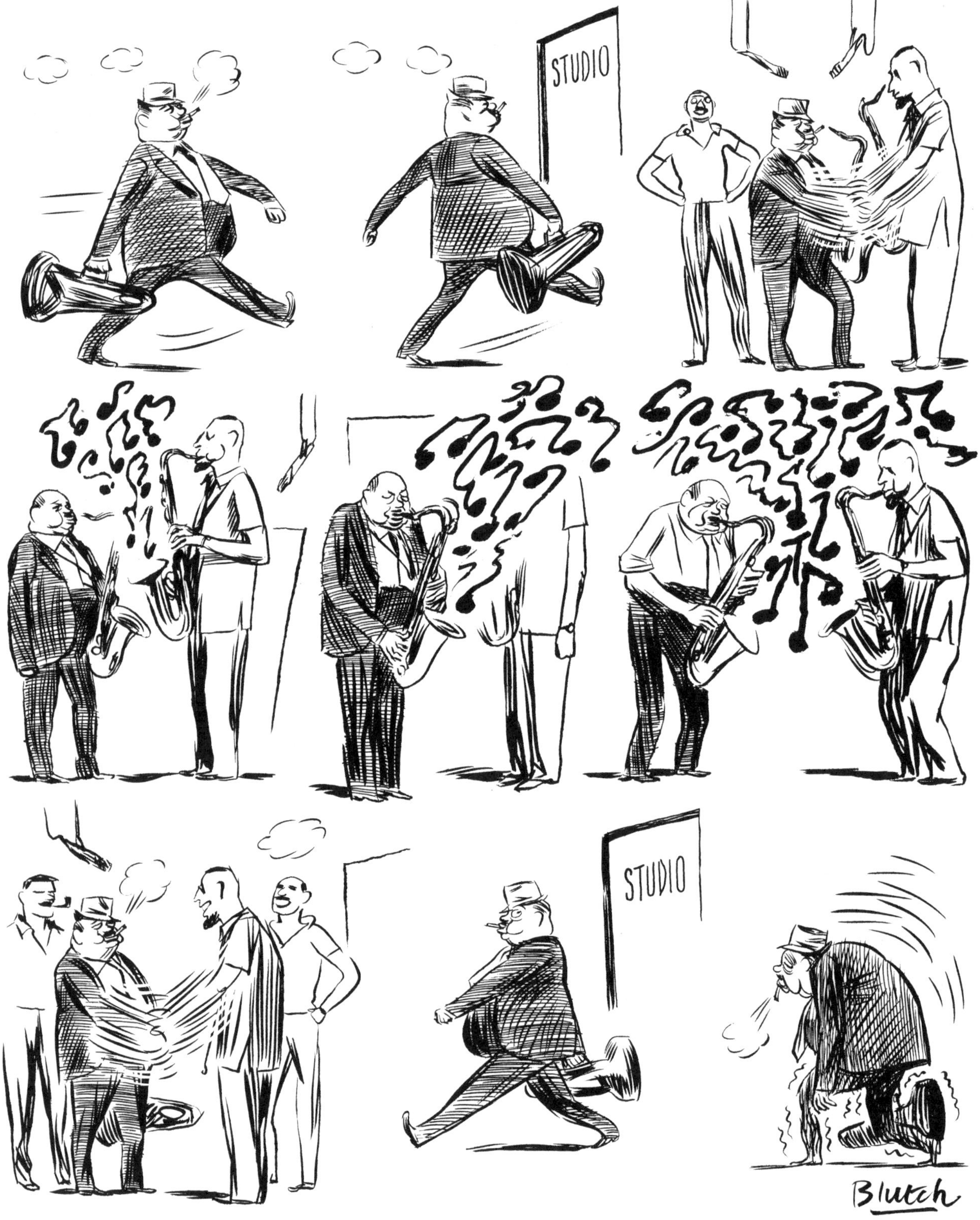
STUDIO
STUDIO
Blutch

sophisticated lady

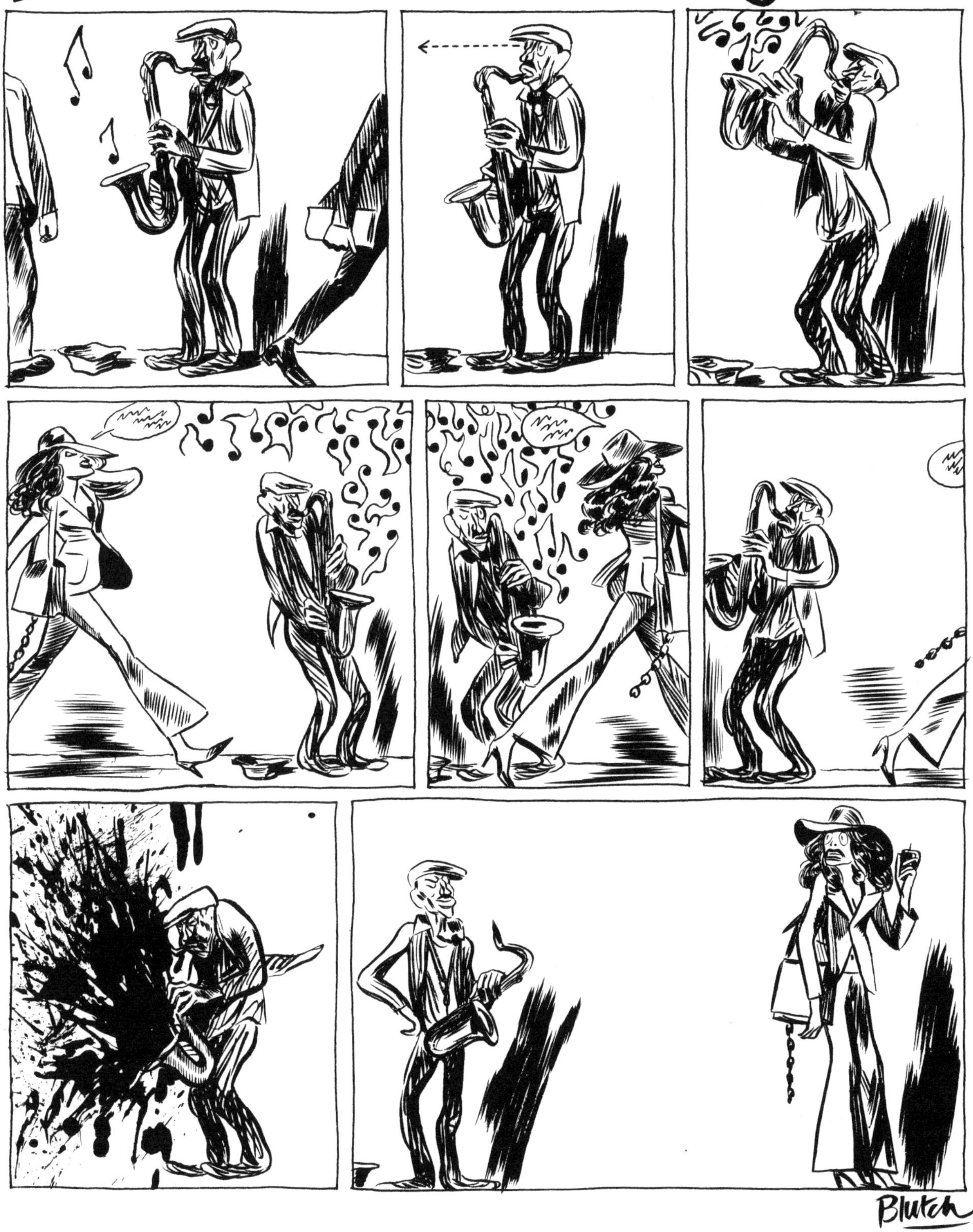
Blutch

She Shot Lee Morgan

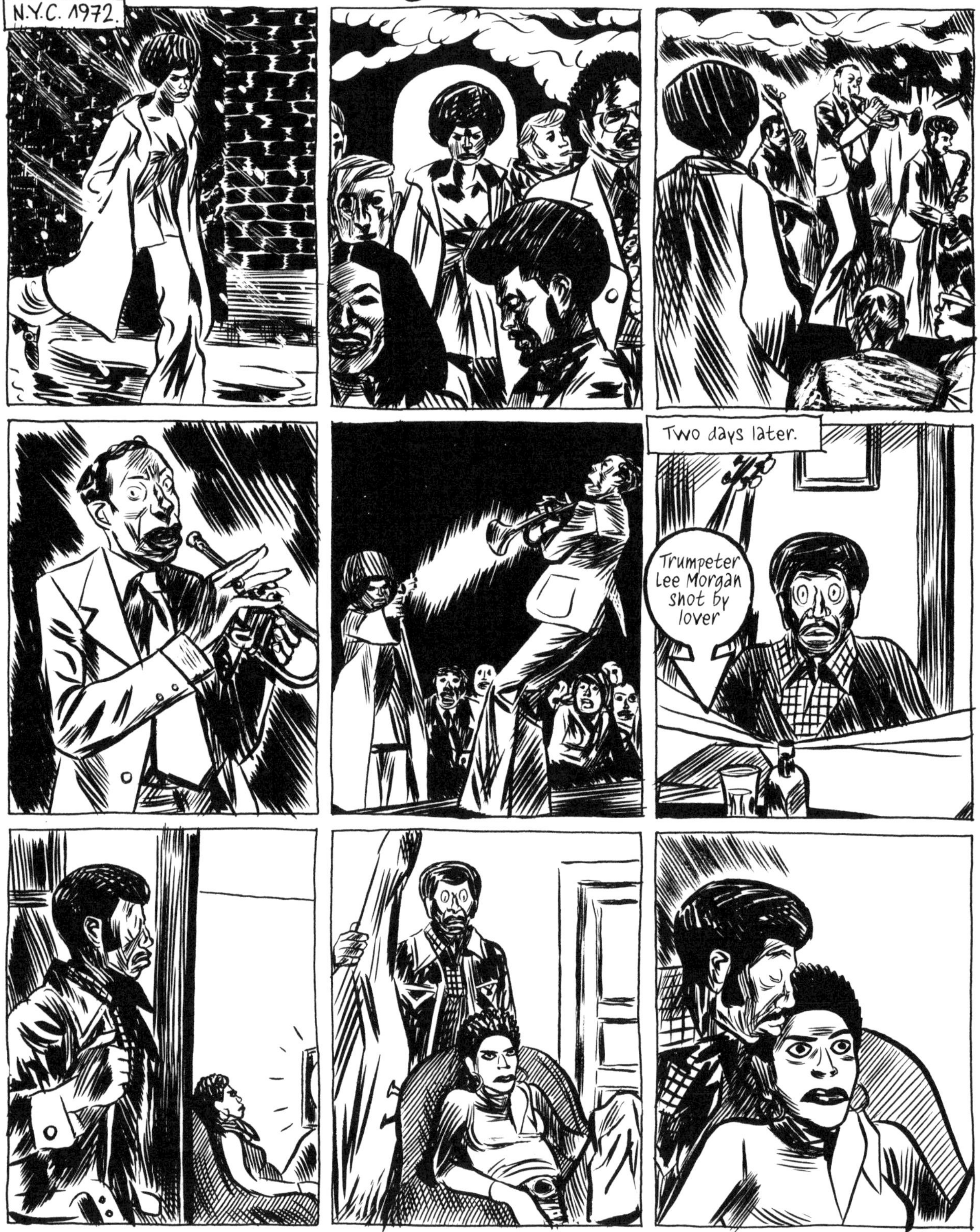

N.Y.C. 1972.
Two days later.
Trumpeter Lee Morgan shot by lover
Blutch

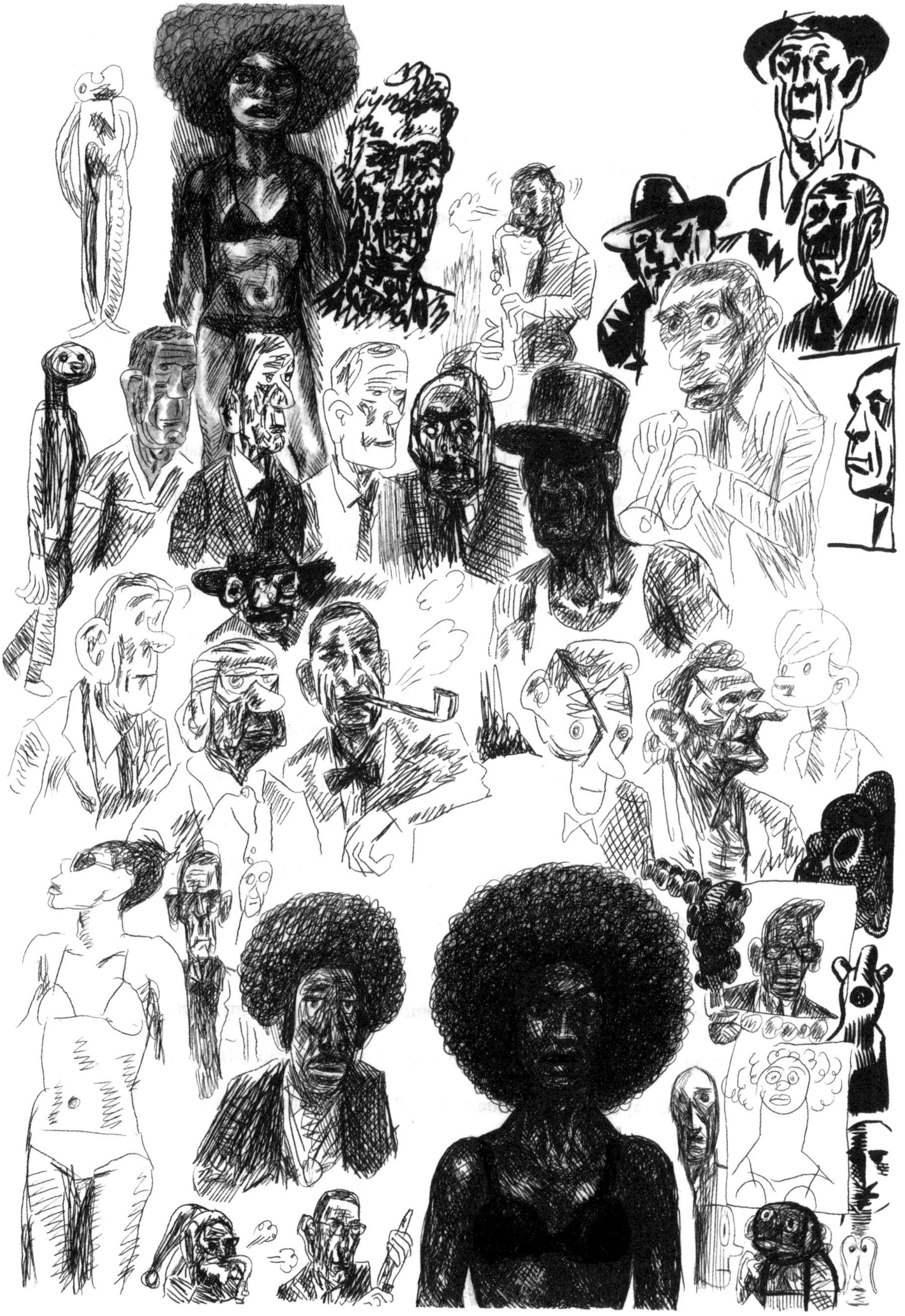

the Life of the artist 2

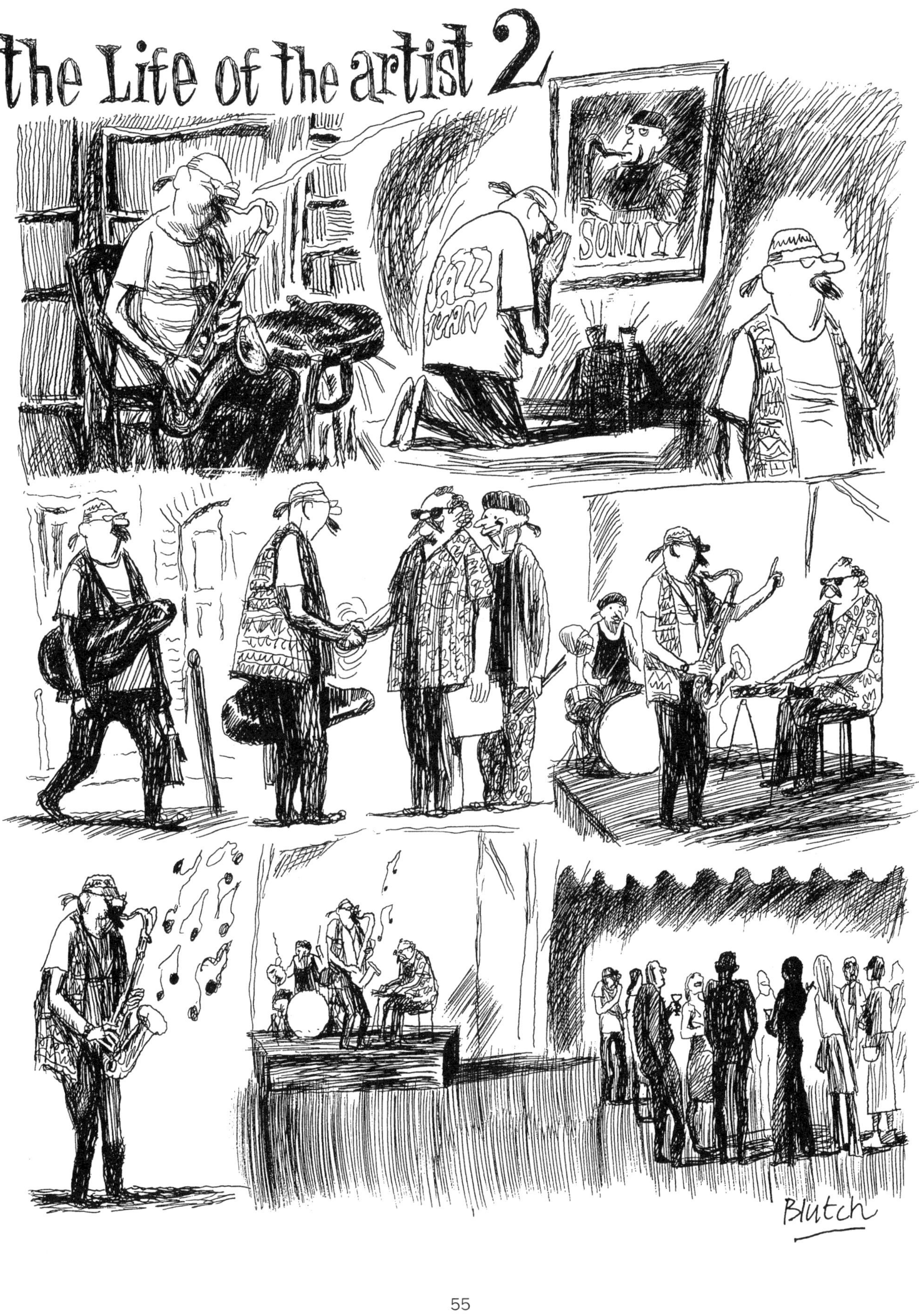
SONNY
JAZZ MAN
Blutch

Marciac festival
a jazz celebration

JAZZ FESTI
Looks like there's nowhere to park...
Just look at this rotten weather...
Downtown
VIVE LE JA
Check out all these idiots! Buncha posers...
It really sucks this year...
MENU JAZZY

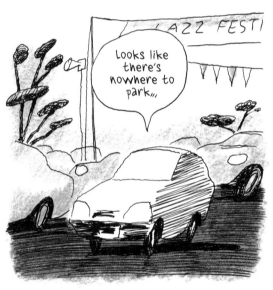

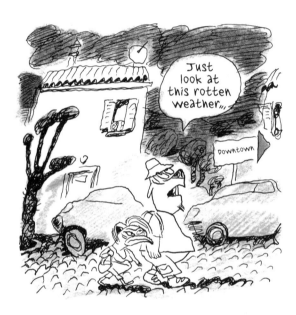

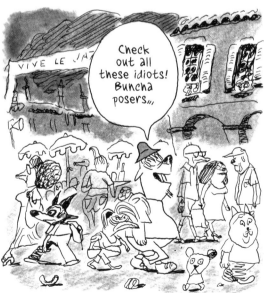

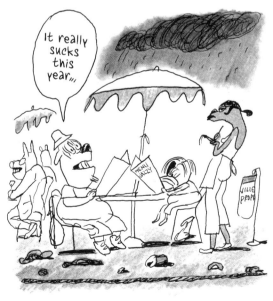

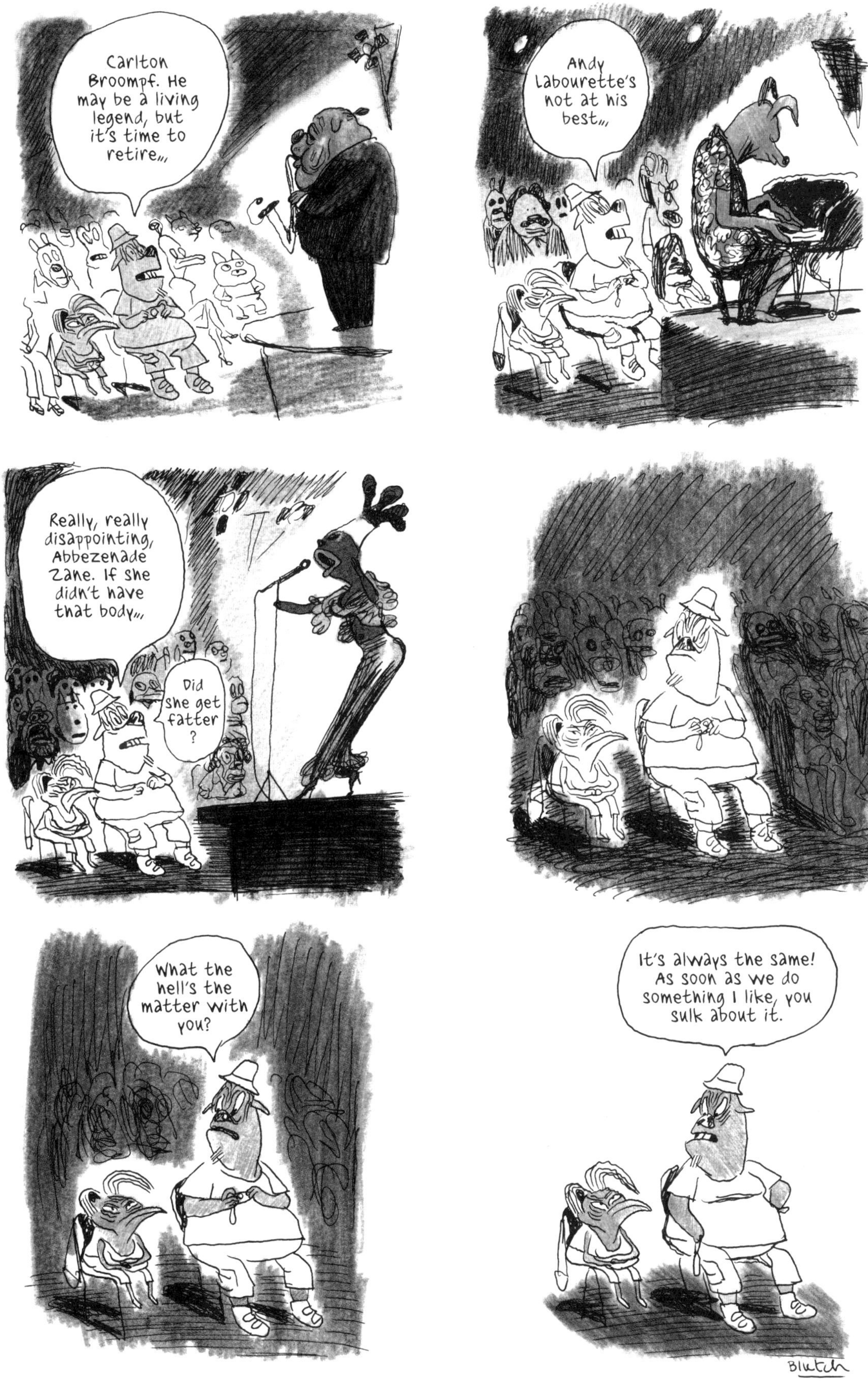
Carlton Broompf. He may be a living legend, but it's time to retire...
Andy Labourette's not at his best...
Really, really disappointing, Abbezenade Zane. If she didn't have that body...
Did she get fatter?
What the hell's the matter with you?
It's always the same! As soon as we do something I like, you sulk about it.
Blutch

MDD III

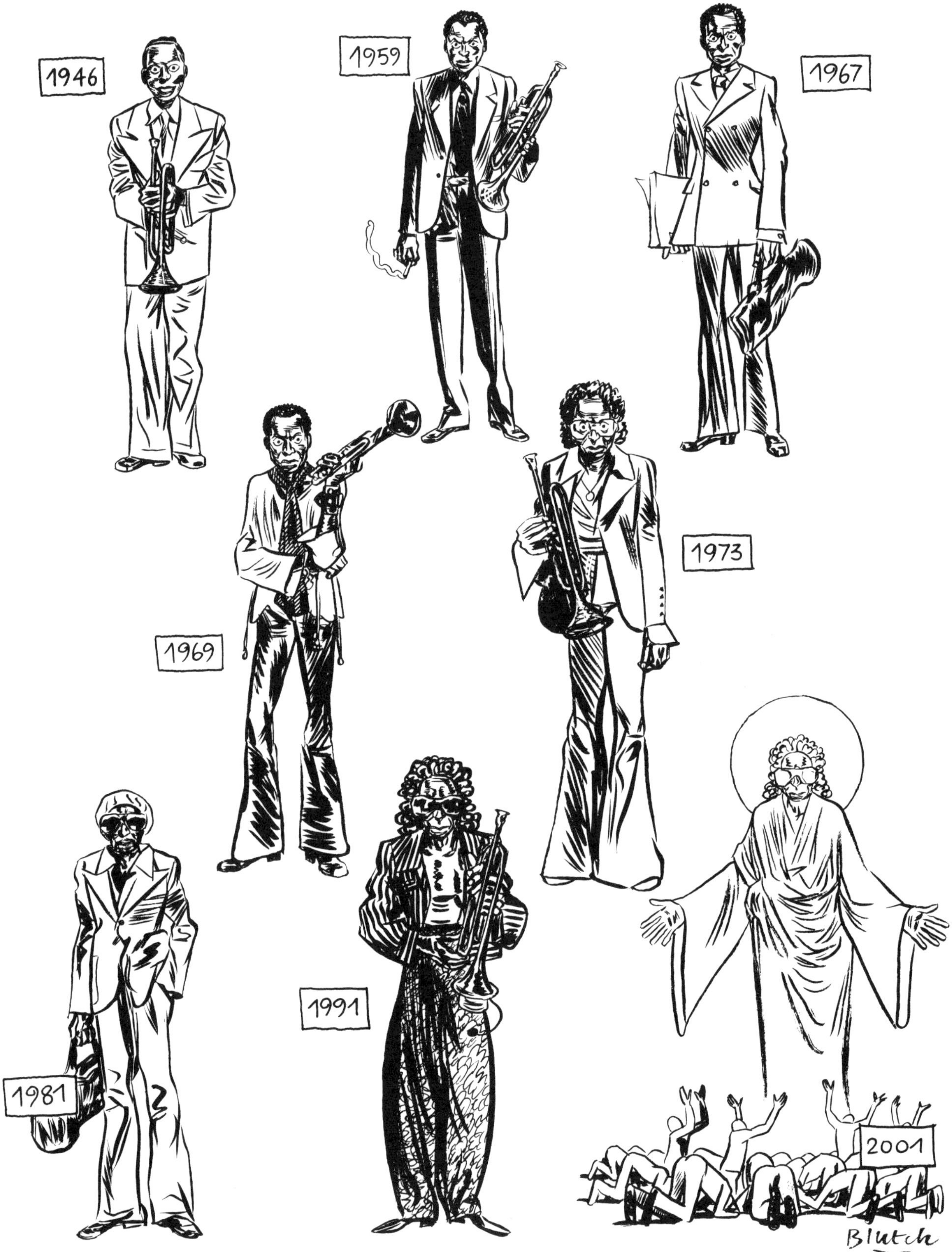
1946
1959
1967
1969
1973
1981
1991
2001
Blutch

diary of a consumer

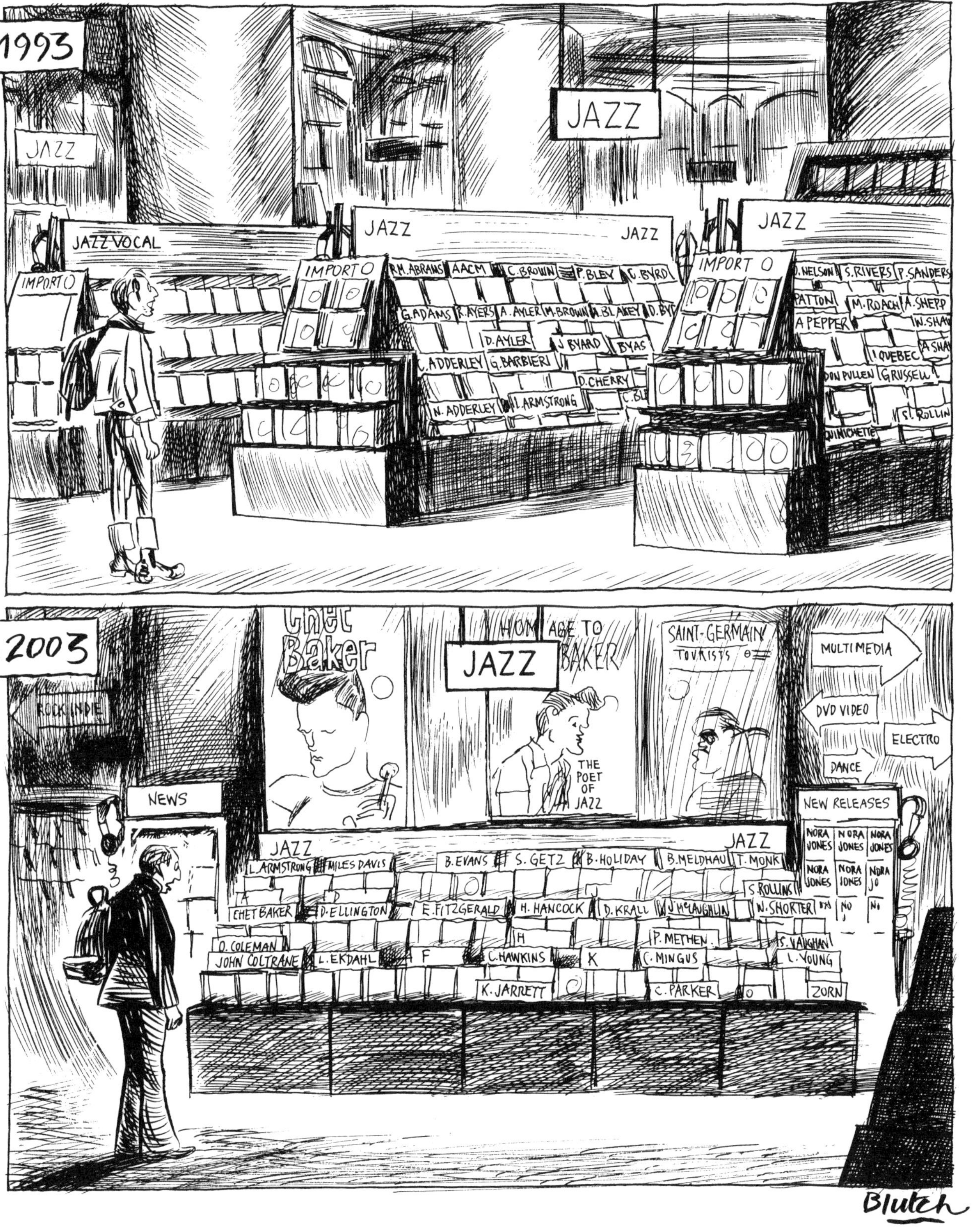
1993
JAZZ
JAZZ
JAZZ VOCAL
IMPORT
JAZZ
JAZZ
JAZZ
IMPORT
R.M. ABRAMS
AACM
C. BROWN
P. BLEY
C. BYRD
G. ADAMS
R. AYERS
A. AYLER
M. BROWN
A. BLAKEY
D. AYLER
J. BYARD
BYAS
C. ADDERLEY
G. BARBIERI
D. CHERRY
N. ADDERLEY
L. ARMSTRONG
IMPORT
S. RIVERS
P. SANDERS
PATTON
M. ROACH
A. SHEPP
A PEPPER
QUEBEC
DON PULLEN
G RUSSELL
S. ROLLIN
QUINICHETTE
2003
ROCK INDIE
SAINT-GERMAIN
TOURISTS
MULTIMEDIA
Chet Baker
JAZZ
DVD VIDEO
ELECTRO
DANCE
THE POET OF JAZZ
NEWS
NEW RELEASES
NORA JONES
NORA JONES
NORA JONES
NORA JONES
NORA JONES
JAZZ
JAZZ
L. ARMSTRONG
MILES DAVIS
B. EVANS
S. GETZ
B. HOLIDAY
B. MELDHAU
T. MONK
S. ROLLINS
CHET BAKER
D. ELLINGTON
E. FITZGERALD
H. HANCOCK
D. KRALL
J. McLAUGHLIN
W. SHORTER
H
P. METHEN
S. VAUGHAN
O. COLEMAN
JOHN COLTRANE
L. EKDAHL
F
C. HAWKINS
K
C. MINGUS
L. YOUNG
K. JARRETT
C. PARKER
ZORN
Blutch

inheritance

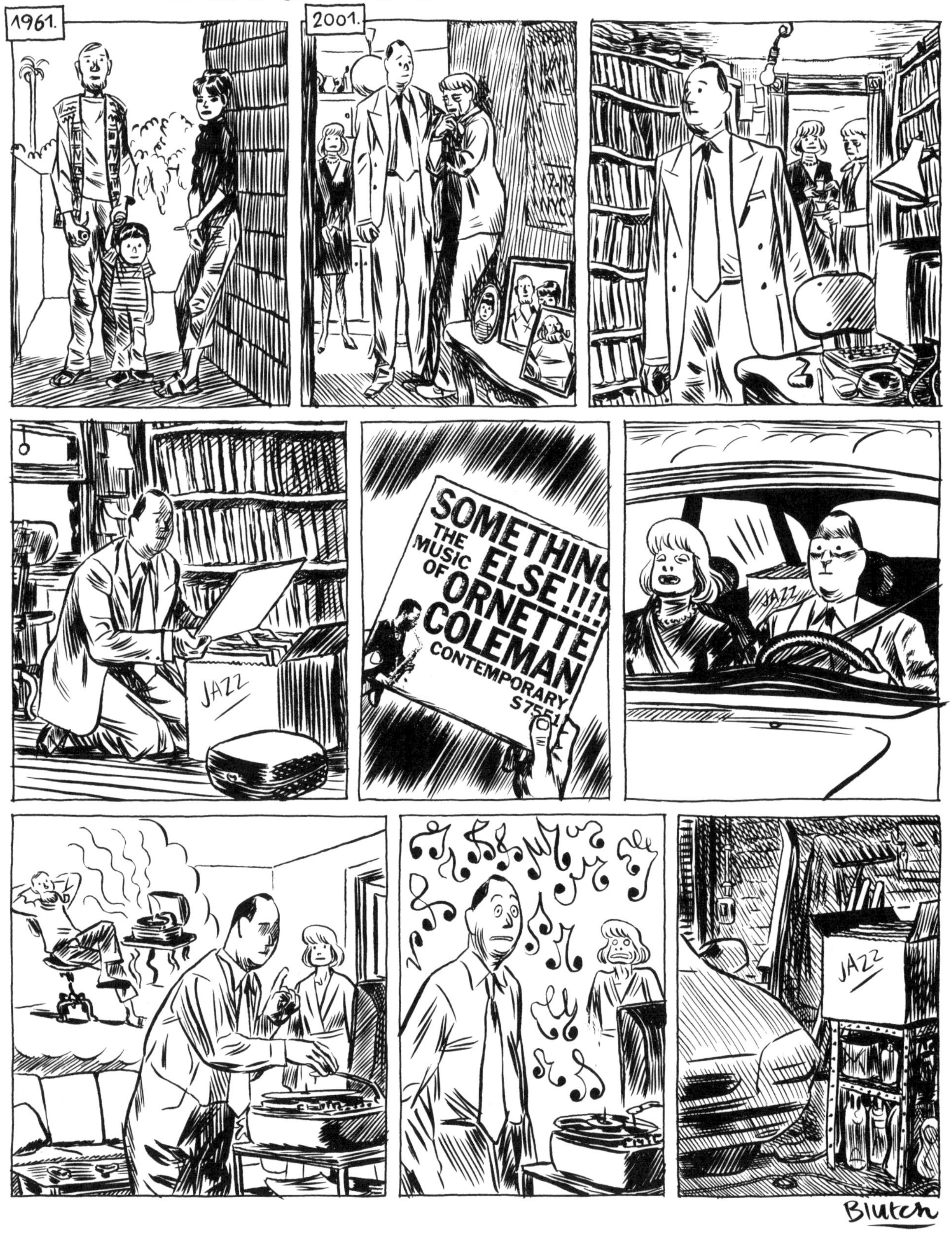
1961.
2001.
SOMETHING ELSE!!!! THE MUSIC OF ORNETTE COLEMAN
CONTEMPORARY
JAZZ
JAZZ
JAZZ
Blutch

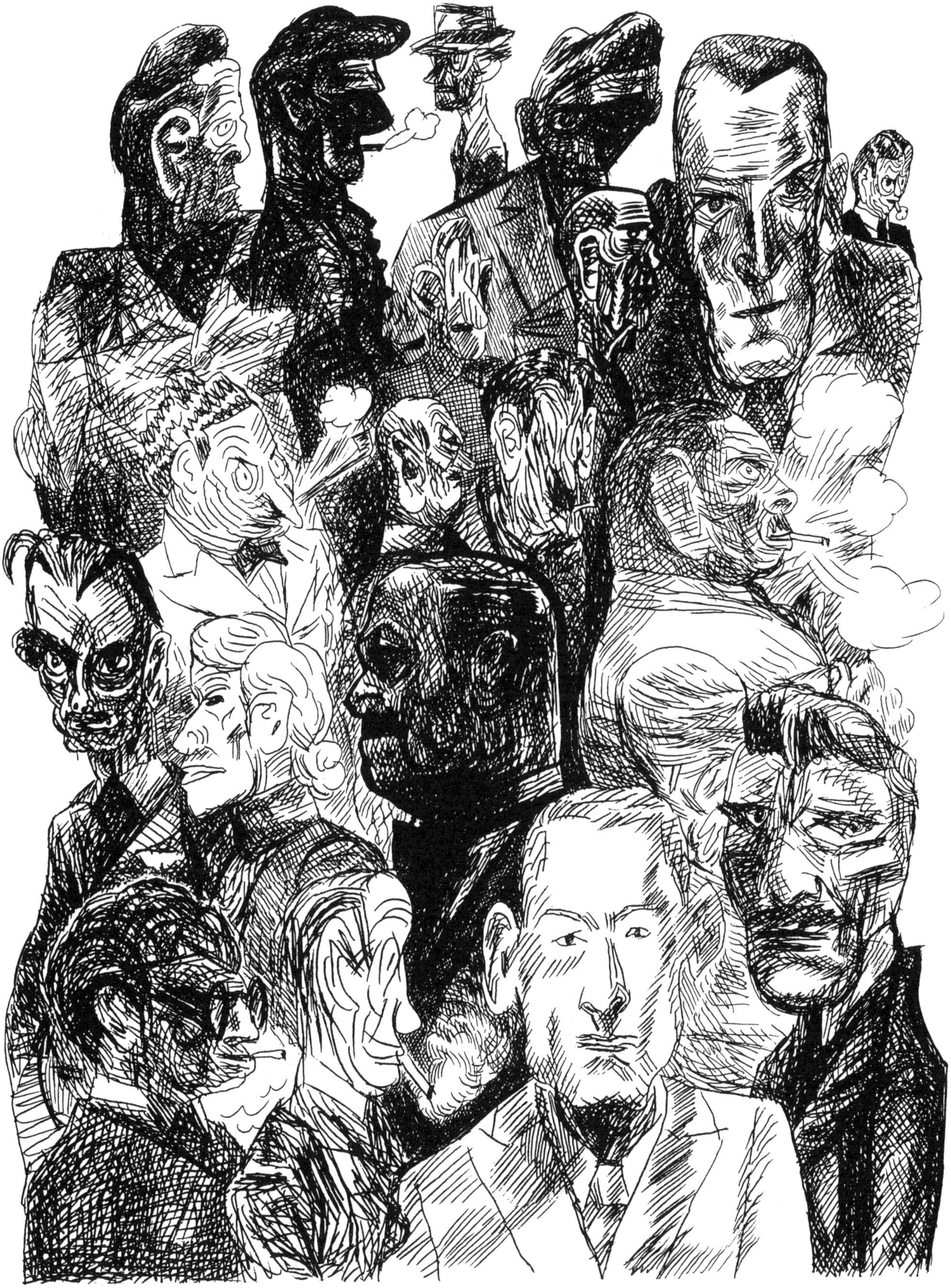

Battling Mingus

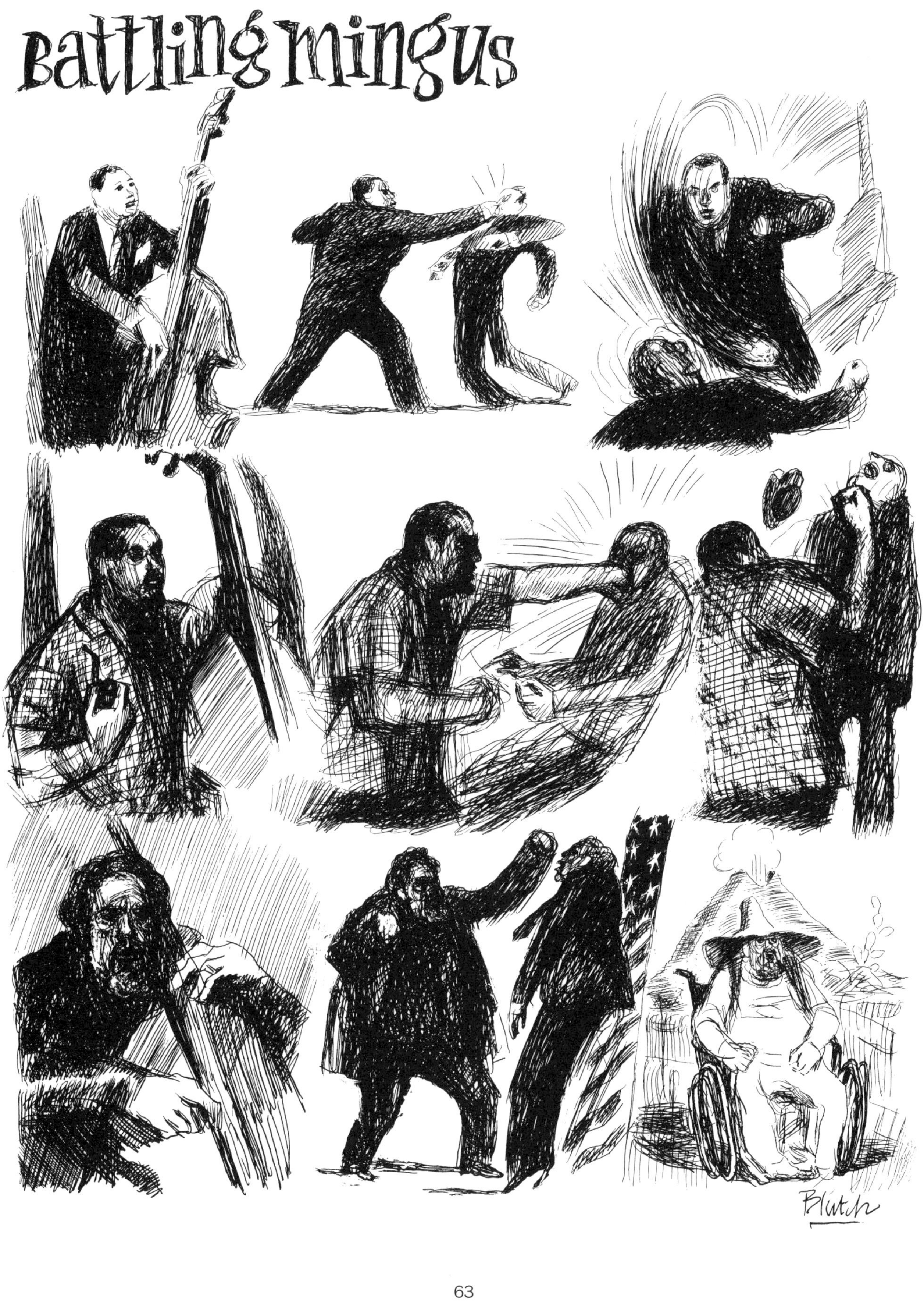

Blutch

the secret life of Sun Ra

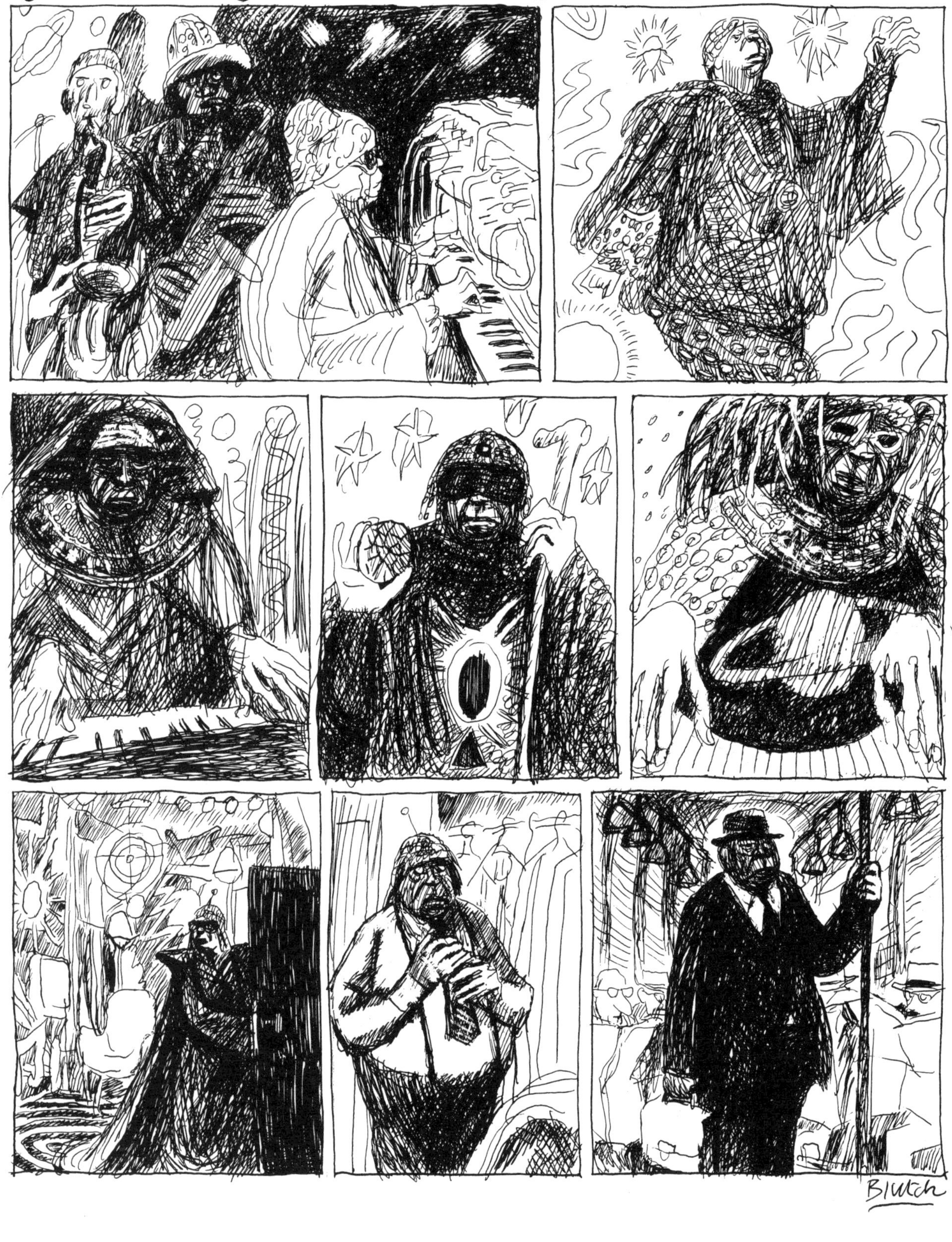

Blutch

the curve of your sax

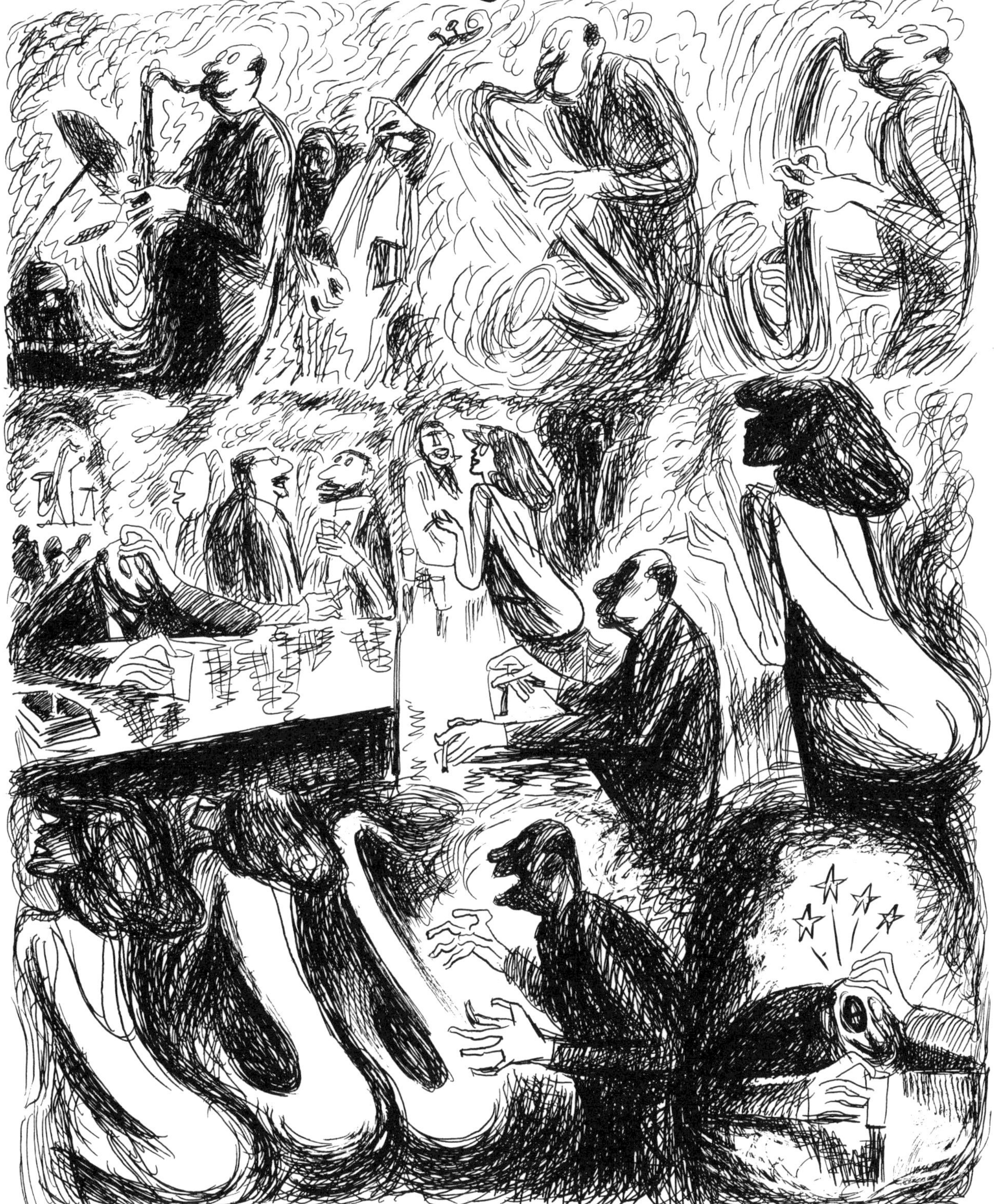

Blutch

the Ghost

(in memory of Chet Baker)

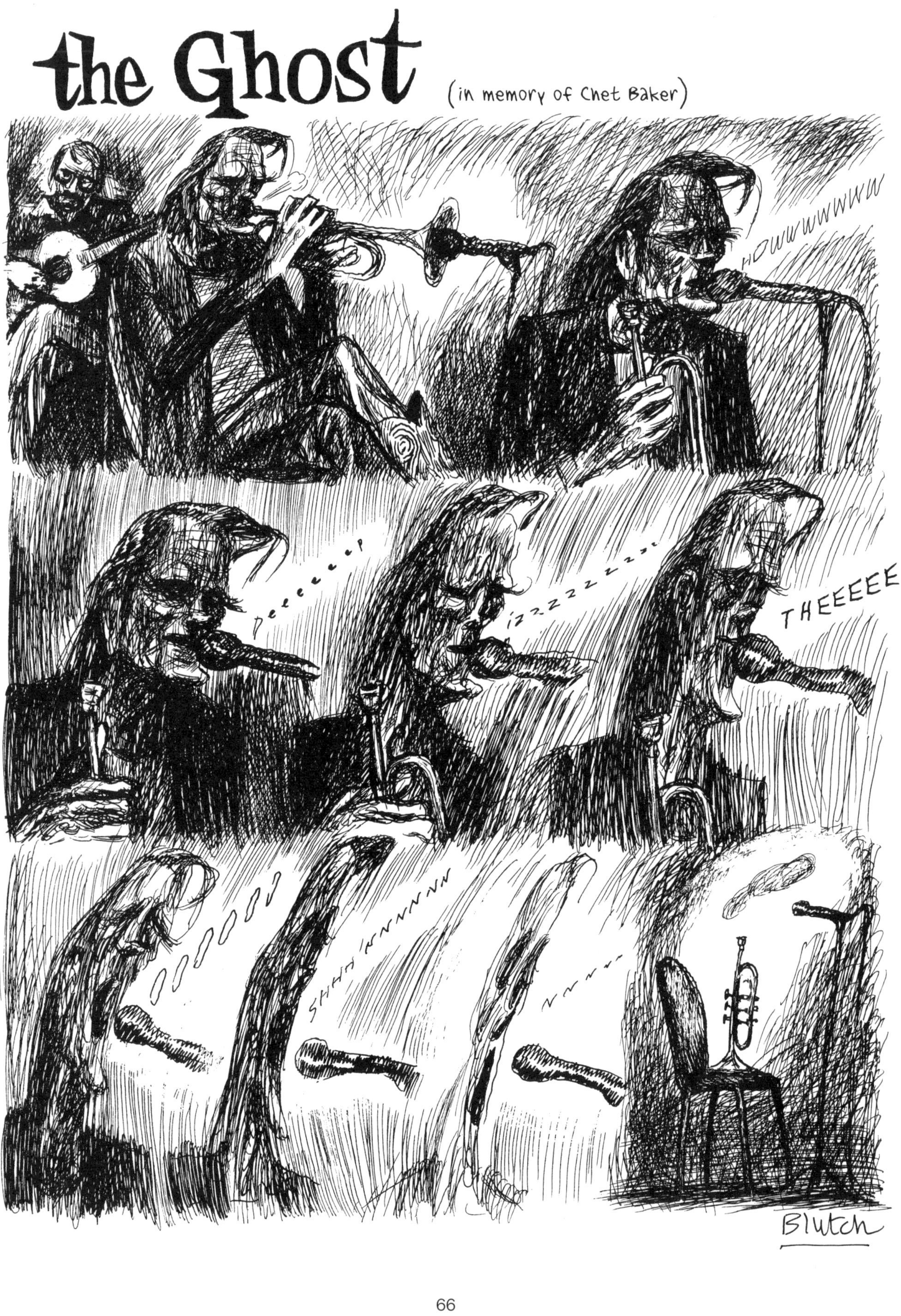
HOWWWWWWWWW
peeeeeeep
izzzzzzzzzzz
THEEEEE
OOOOOOOO
SHHH'NNNNNNNN
NNNNN

Blutch

music is my mistress (The End Suite)

Columbia Presbyterian Medical Center. NYC. May 24, 1974.

Blutch

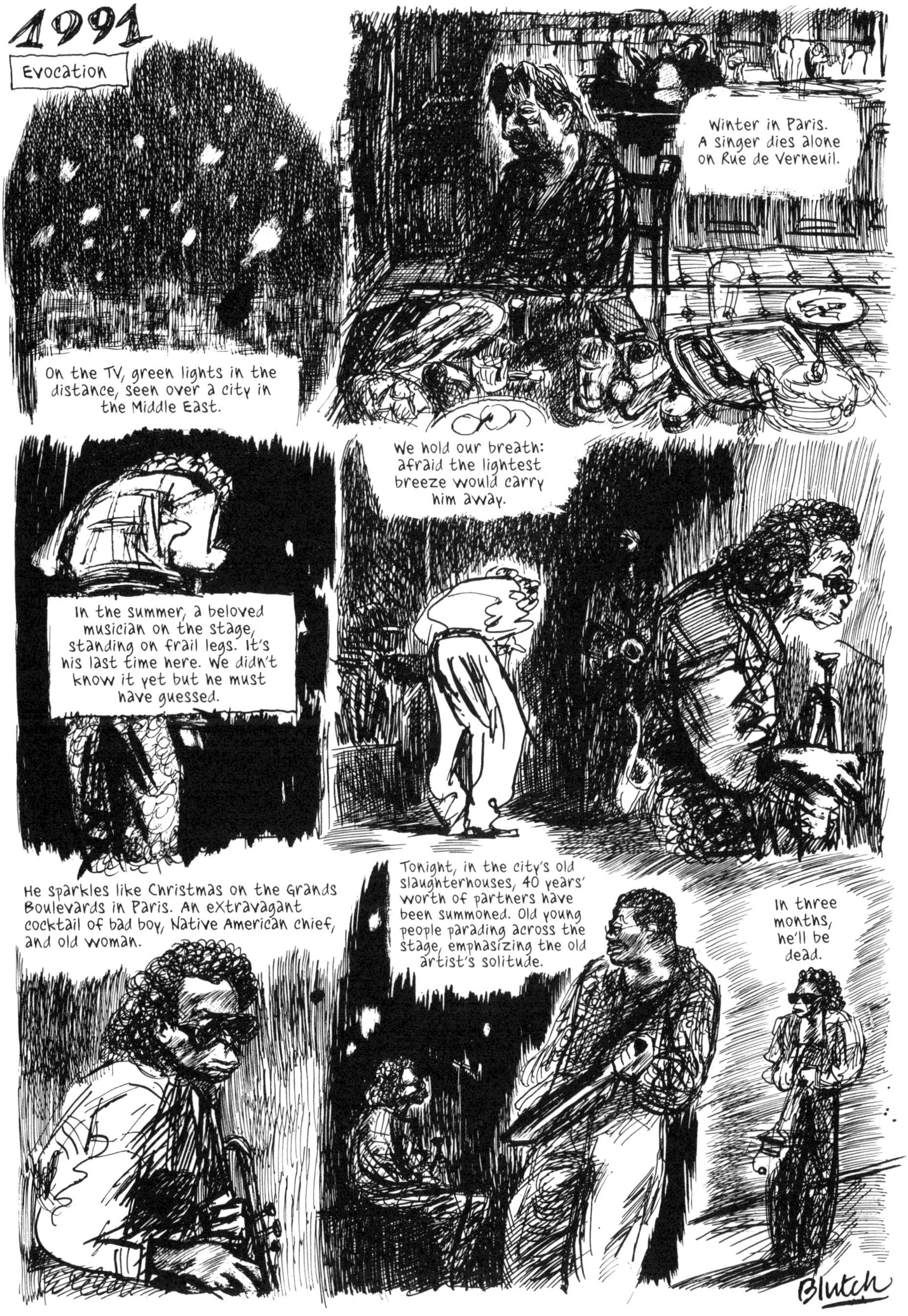
1991
Evocation
On the TV, green lights in the distance, seen over a city in the Middle East.
Winter in Paris. A singer dies alone on Rue de Verneuil.
In the summer, a beloved musician on the stage, standing on frail legs. It's his last time here. We didn't know it yet but he must have guessed.
We hold our breath: afraid the lightest breeze would carry him away.
He sparkles like Christmas on the Grands Boulevards in Paris. An extravagant cocktail of bad boy, Native American chief, and old woman.
Tonight, in the city's old slaughterhouses, 40 years' worth of partners have been summoned. Old young people parading across the stage, emphasizing the old artist's solitude.
In three months, he'll be dead.
Blutch

the abstract truth

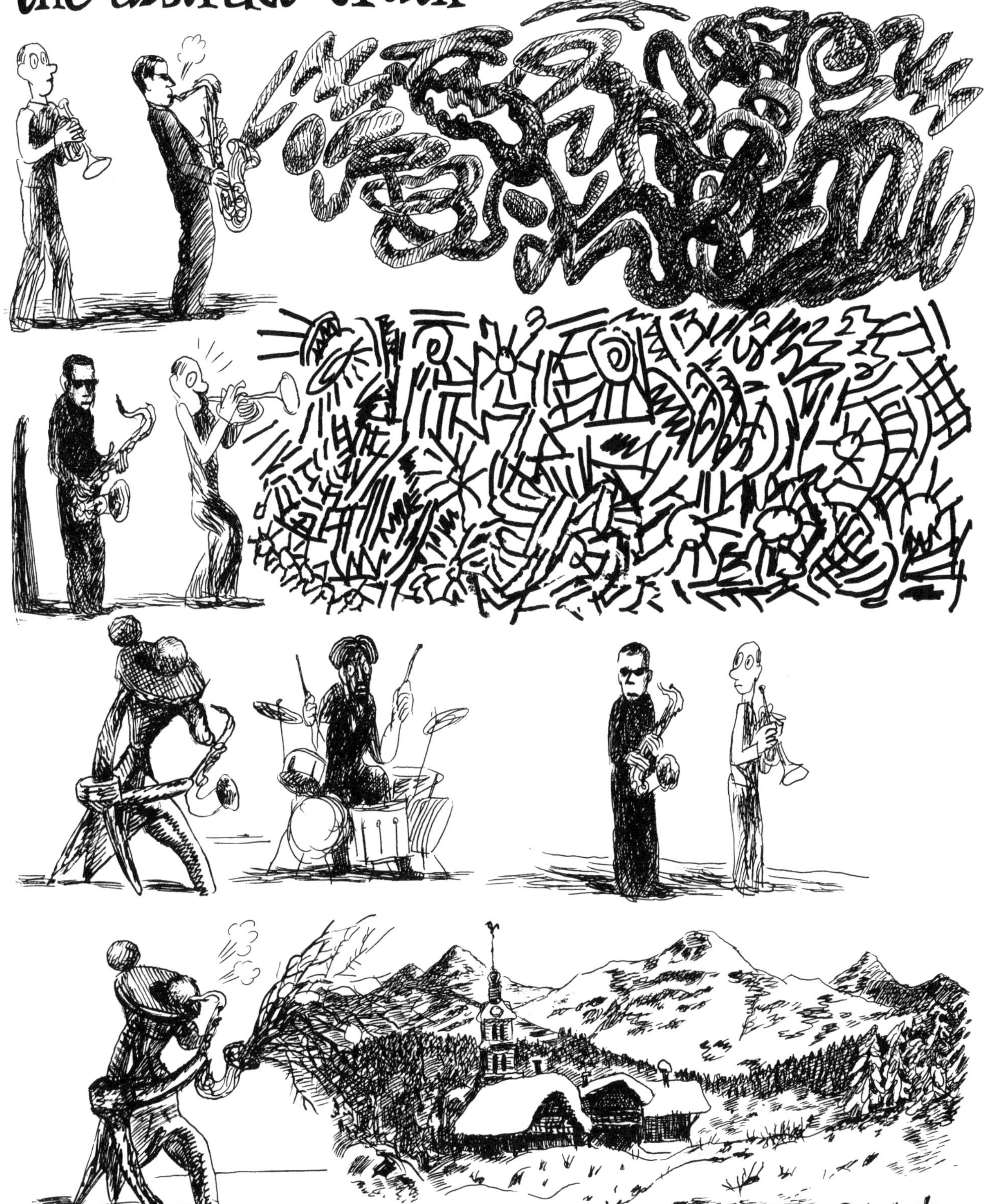
Blutch

viva italia!

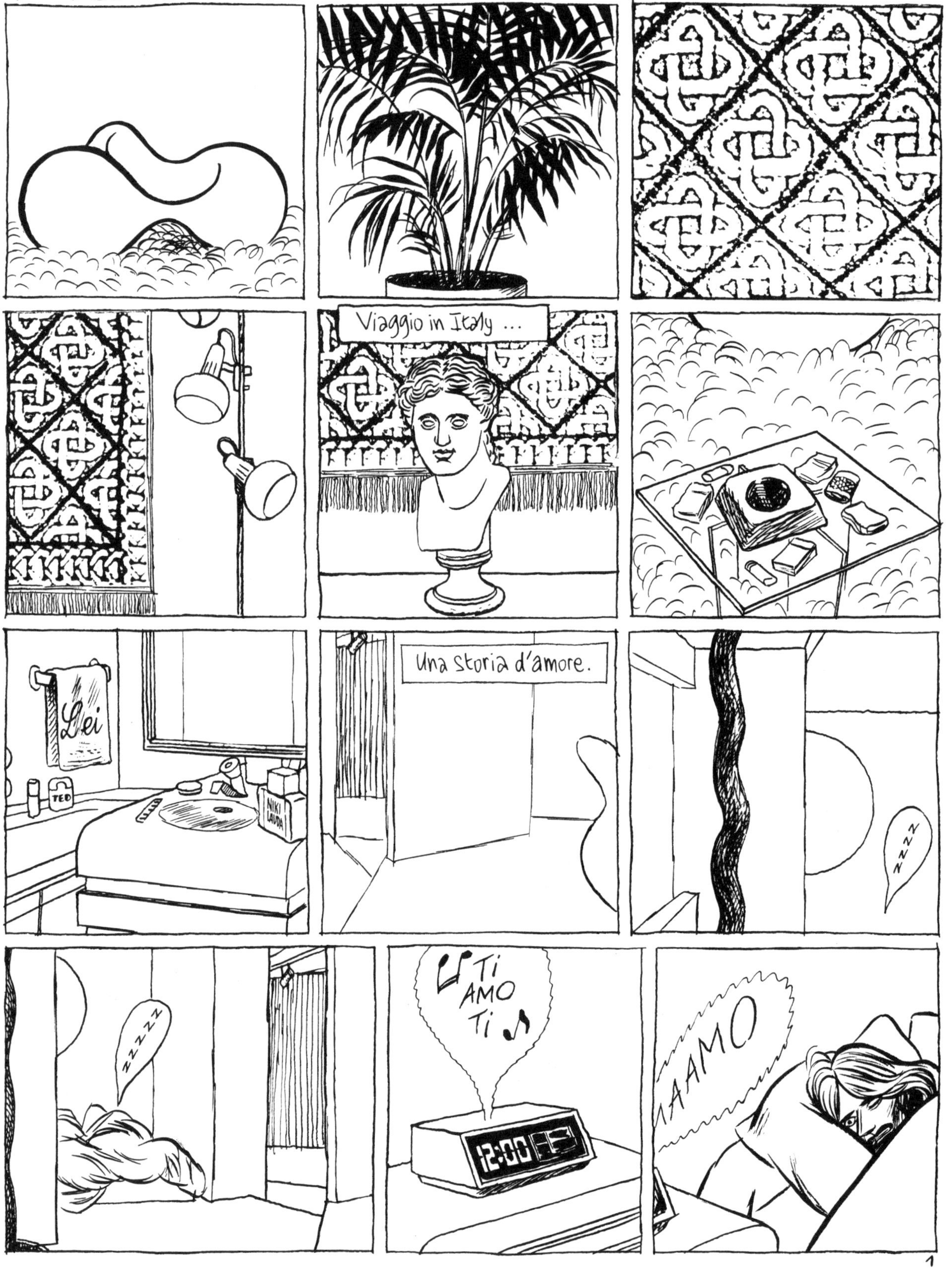
Viaggio in Italy ...
Lei
TED
NIKI LAUDA
Una storia d'amore.
zzzz
zzzzz
Ti AMO Ti
12:00
AAMO

1

The gladiators enter.
Ti AMO Ti AMO
ZZZZZZ
ZZZZZ
CiAO CARLO!
CiAO RiCCARDO!
CiAO UMBERTO!
CiAO RiCCARDO!
CiAO CARLO!
CiAO UMBERTO!
Ti AMO Ti
HAHAHAHAHA
HAHAHAHA
HAHAHA HAHA
DING DONG
DING
MOMENTO!

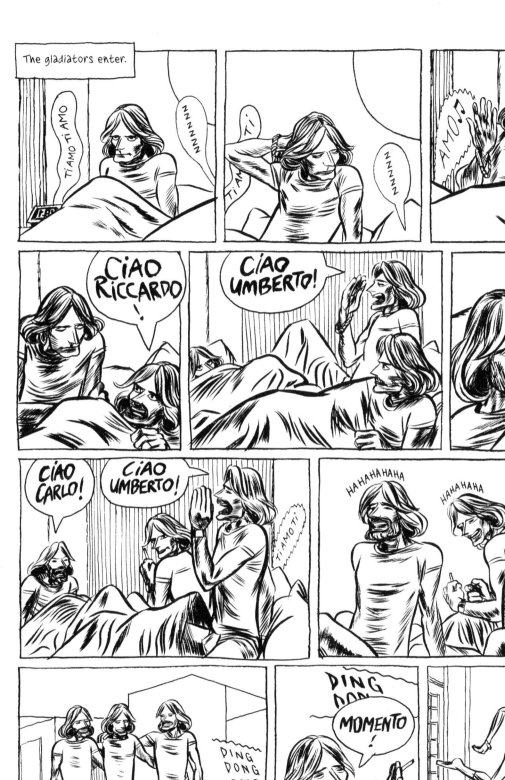

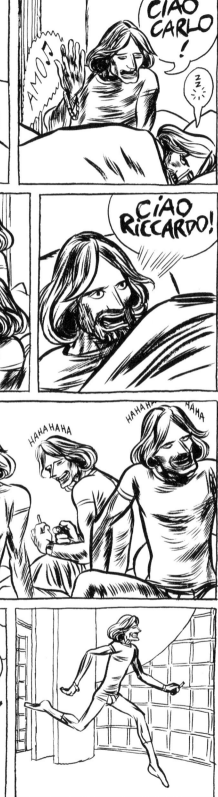

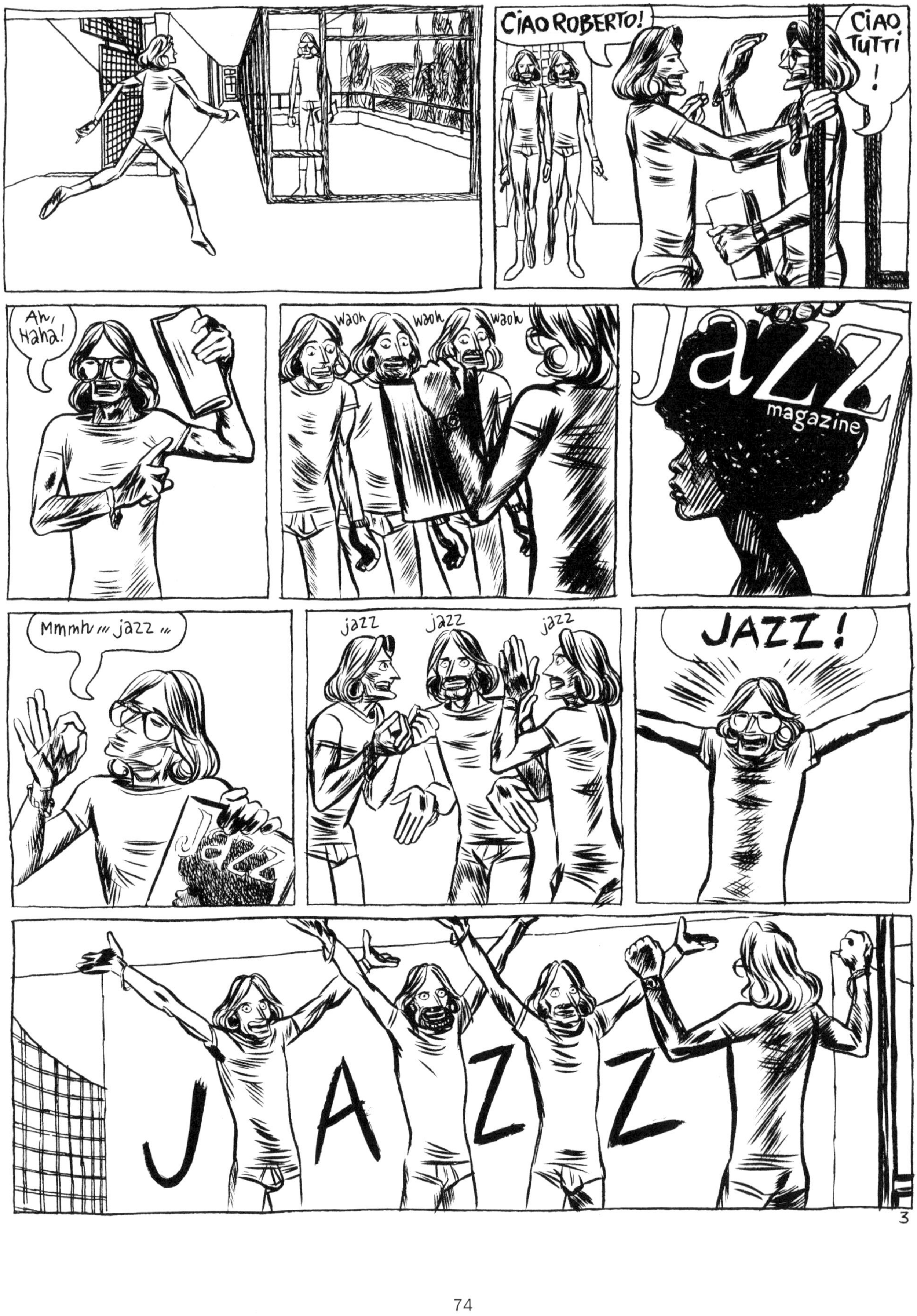
CIAO ROBERTO!
CIAO TUTTI !
Ah, Haha!
waoh
waoh
waoh
jazz
magazine
Mmmh ,,, jazz ,,,
jazz
jazz
jazz
JAZZ!
JAZZ

3

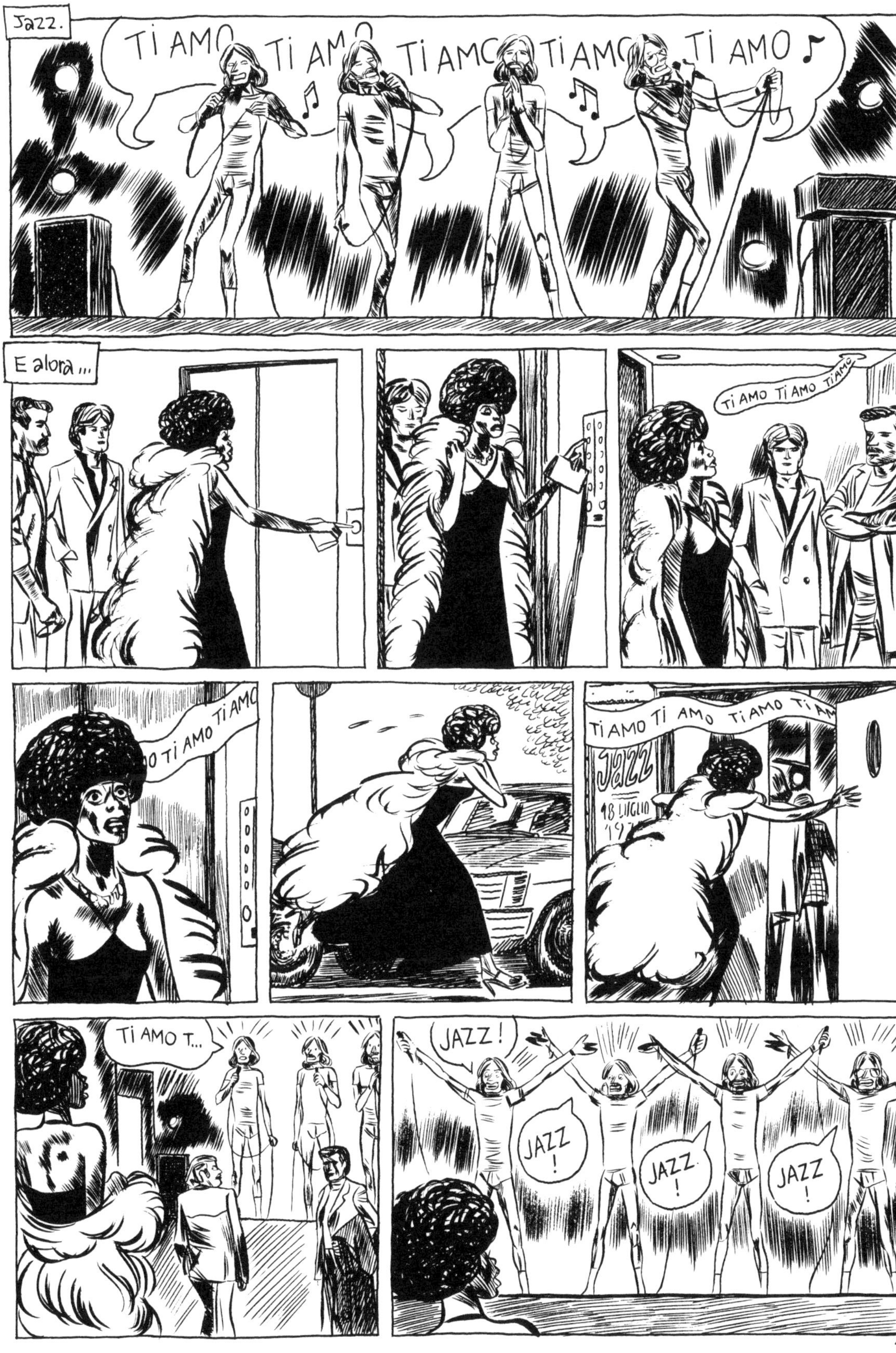
Jazz.
TI AMO TI AMO TI AMO TI AMO TI AMO ♪
E alora...
TI AMO TI AMO TI AMO
O TI AMO TI AMO
TI AMO TI AMO TI AMO TI A
JAZZ
18 LUGLIO
TI AMO T...
JAZZ!
JAZZ!
JAZZ!
JAZZ!
4

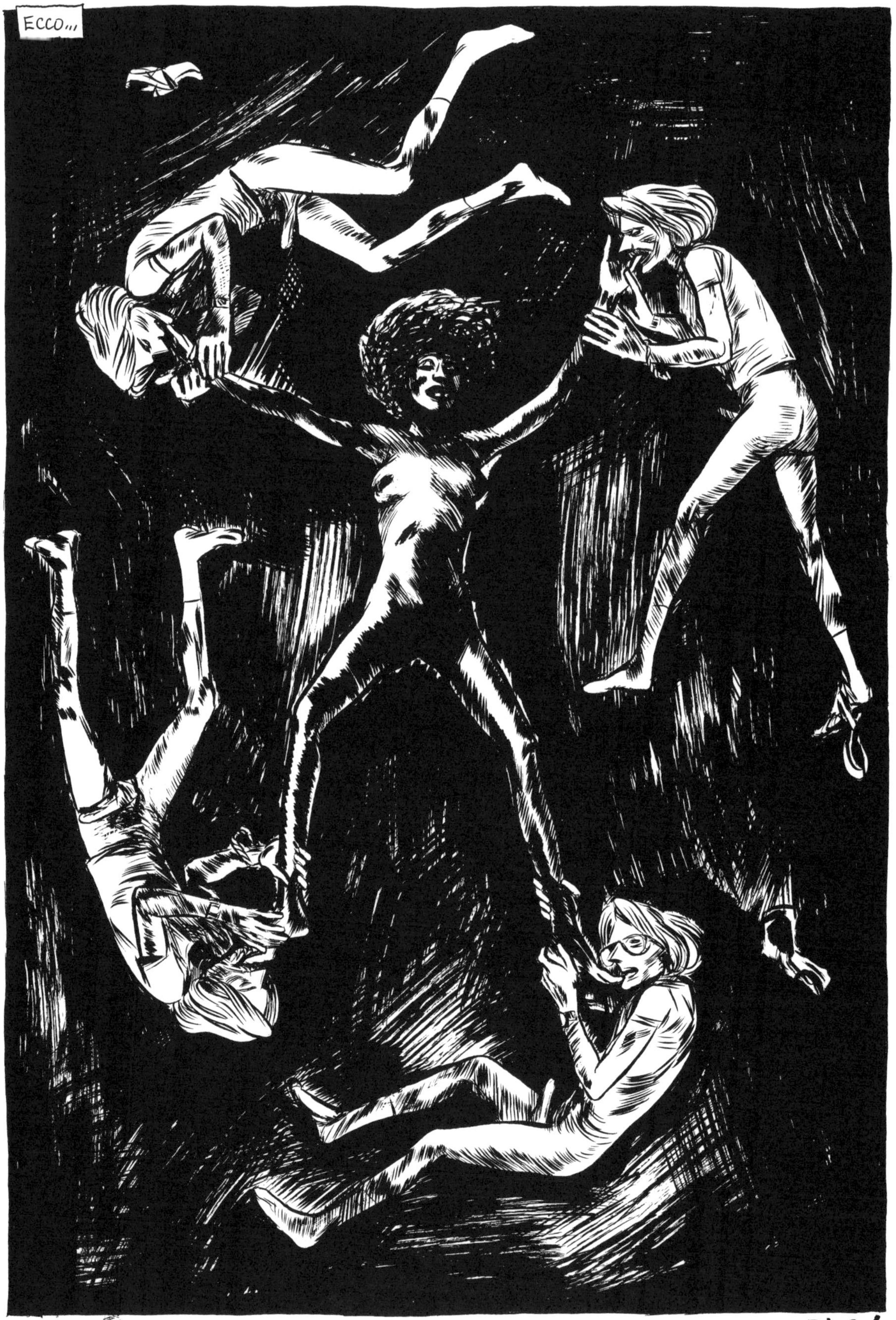
ECCO...

Blutch

lets finish with some JAZZ

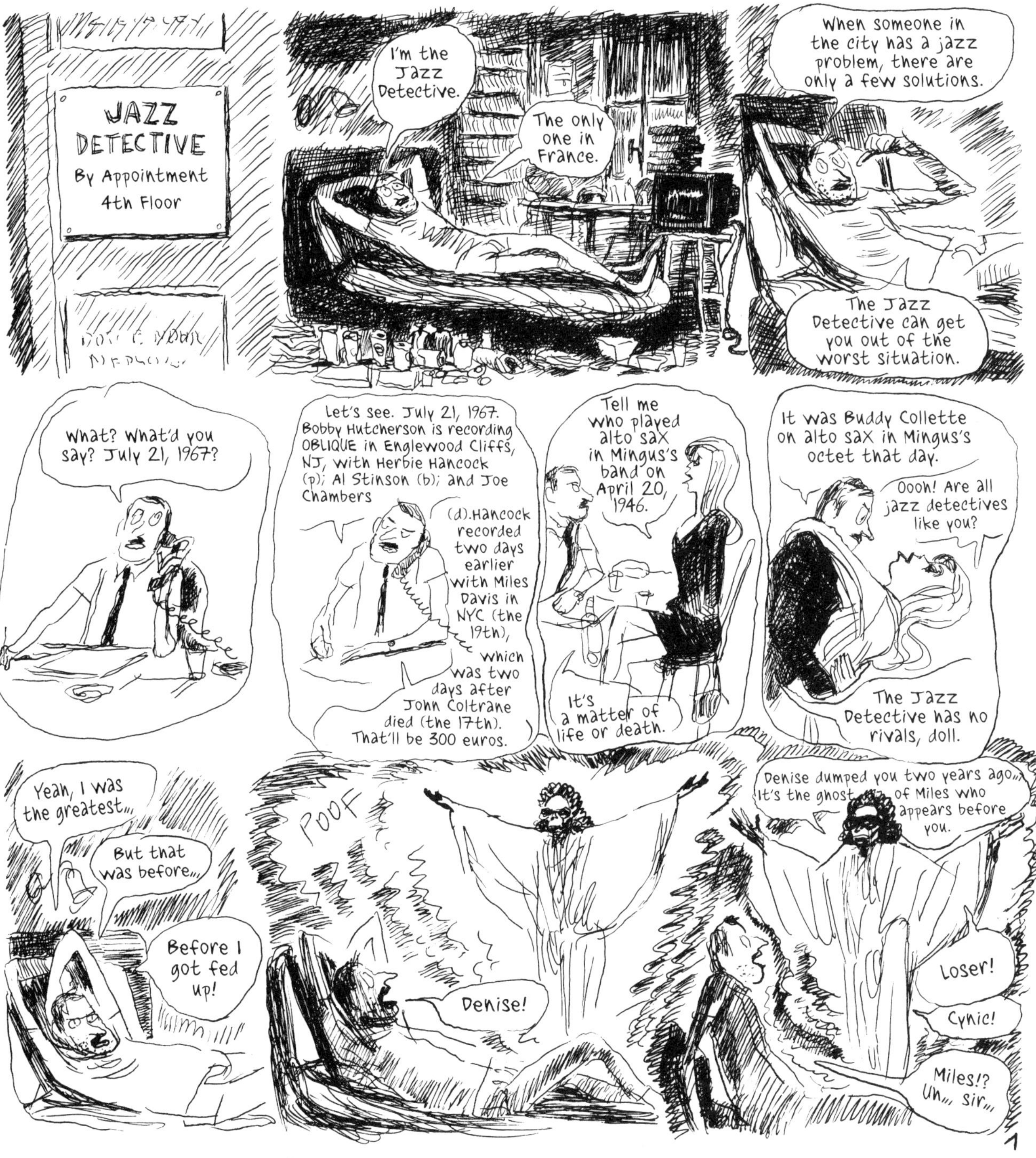
JAZZ DETECTIVE
By Appointment
4th Floor
I'm the Jazz Detective.
The only one in France.
When someone in the city has a jazz problem, there are only a few solutions.
The Jazz Detective can get you out of the worst situation.
What? What'd you say? July 21, 1967?
Let's see. July 21, 1967. Bobby Hutcherson is recording OBLIQUE in Englewood Cliffs, NJ, with Herbie Hancock (p); Al Stinson (b); and Joe Chambers
(d).Hancock recorded two days earlier with Miles Davis in NYC (the 19th),
which was two days after John Coltrane died (the 17th). That'll be 300 euros.
Tell me who played alto sax in Mingus's band on April 20, 1946.
It's a matter of life or death.
It was Buddy Collette on alto sax in Mingus's octet that day.
Oooh! Are all jazz detectives like you?
The Jazz Detective has no rivals, doll.
Yeah, I was the greatest...
But that was before...
Before I got fed up!
POOF
Denise!
Denise dumped you two years ago... It's the ghost of Miles who appears before you.
Loser!
Cynic!
Miles!? Uh... sir...

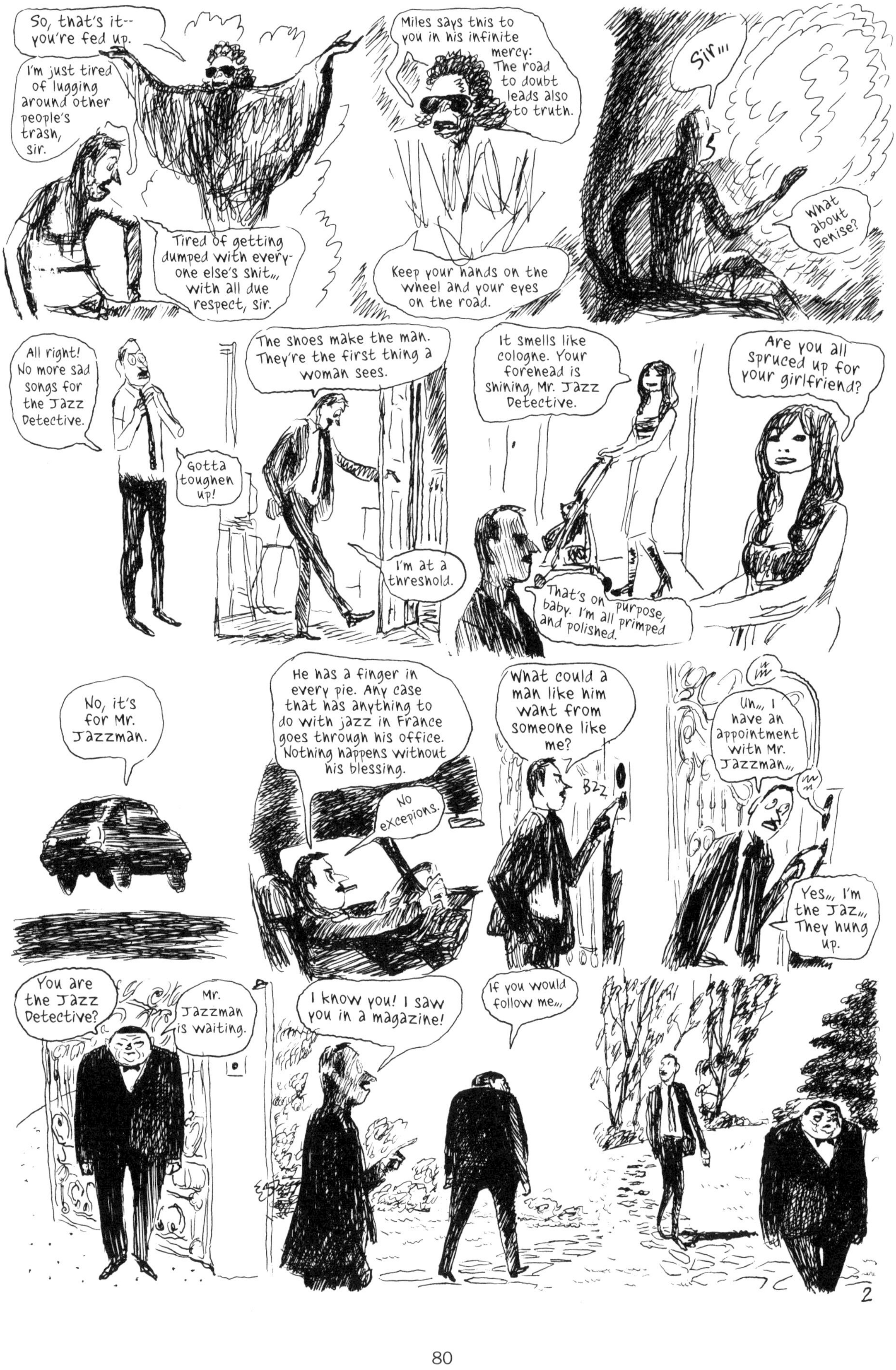
So, that's it-- you're fed up.
I'm just tired of lugging around other people's trash, sir.
Tired of getting dumped with every-one else's shit,,, with all due respect, sir.
Miles says this to you in his infinite mercy: The road to doubt leads also to truth.
Keep your hands on the wheel and your eyes on the road.
Sir,,,
What about Denise?
All right! No more sad songs for the Jazz Detective.
Gotta toughen up!
The shoes make the man. They're the first thing a woman sees.
I'm at a threshold.
It smells like cologne. Your forehead is shining, Mr. Jazz Detective.
That's on purpose, baby. I'm all primped and polished.
Are you all spruced up for your girlfriend?
No, it's for Mr. Jazzman.
He has a finger in every pie. Any case that has anything to do with jazz in France goes through his office. Nothing happens without his blessing.
No excepions.
What could a man like him want from someone like me?
BZZ
Uh,,, I have an appointment with Mr. Jazzman,,,
Yes,,, I'm the Jaz,,, They hung up.
You are the Jazz Detective?
Mr. Jazzman is waiting.
I know you! I saw you in a magazine!
If you would follow me,,,
2

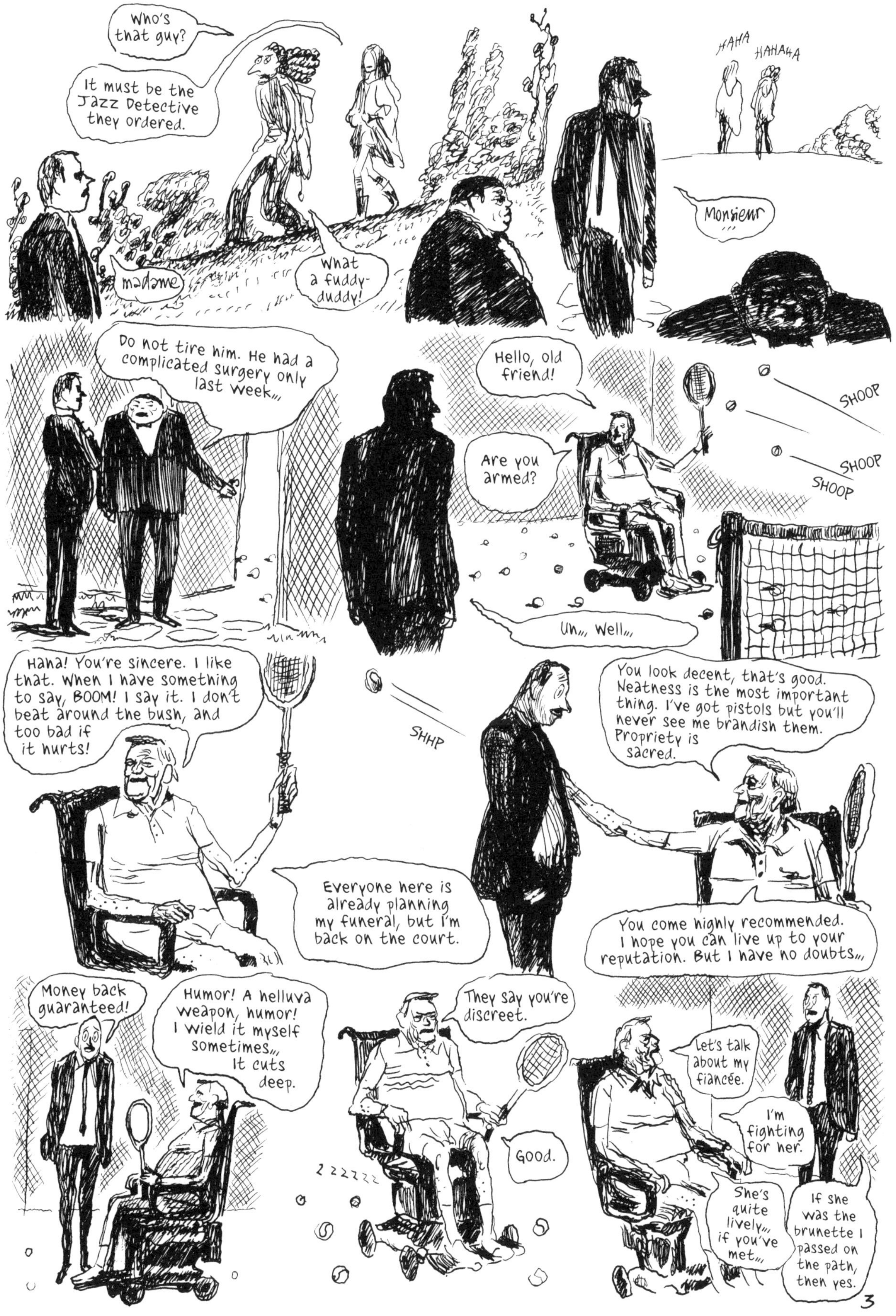
Who's that guy?
It must be the Jazz Detective they ordered.
madame
What a fuddy-duddy!
HAHA
HAHAHA
Monsieur
Do not tire him. He had a complicated surgery only last week...
Hello, old friend!
SHOOP
SHOOP
SHOOP
Are you armed?
Uh... Well...
Haha! You're sincere. I like that. When I have something to say, BOOM! I say it. I don't beat around the bush, and too bad if it hurts!
SHHP
You look decent, that's good. Neatness is the most important thing. I've got pistols but you'll never see me brandish them. Propriety is sacred.
Everyone here is already planning my funeral, but I'm back on the court.
You come highly recommended. I hope you can live up to your reputation. But I have no doubts...
Money back guaranteed!
Humor! A helluva weapon, humor! I wield it myself sometimes... It cuts deep.
They say you're discreet.
Good.
ZZZZZZ
Let's talk about my fiancée.
I'm fighting for her.
She's quite lively... if you've met...
If she was the brunette I passed on the path, then yes.
3

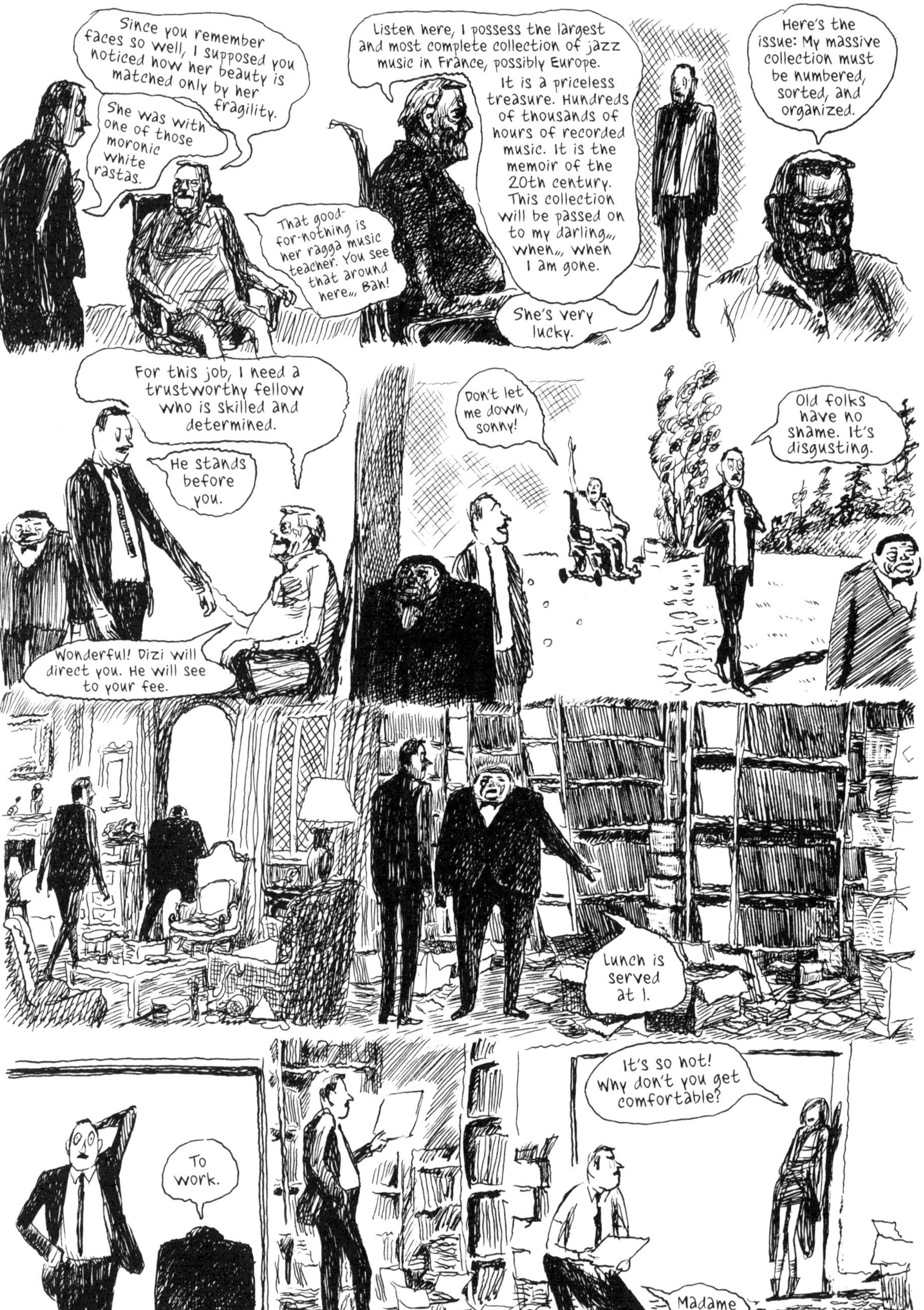

Since you remember faces so well, I supposed you noticed how her beauty is matched only by her fragility.
She was with one of those moronic white rastas.
That good-for-nothing is her ragga music teacher. You see that around here... Bah!
Listen here, I possess the largest and most complete collection of jazz music in France, possibly Europe.
It is a priceless treasure. Hundreds of thousands of hours of recorded music. It is the memoir of the 20th century. This collection will be passed on to my darling... when... when I am gone.
She's very lucky.
Here's the issue: My massive collection must be numbered, sorted, and organized.
For this job, I need a trustworthy fellow who is skilled and determined.
He stands before you.
Wonderful! Dizi will direct you. He will see to your fee.
Don't let me down, sonny!
Old folks have no shame. It's disgusting.
Lunch is served at 1.
To work.
It's so hot! Why don't you get comfortable?
Madame
4

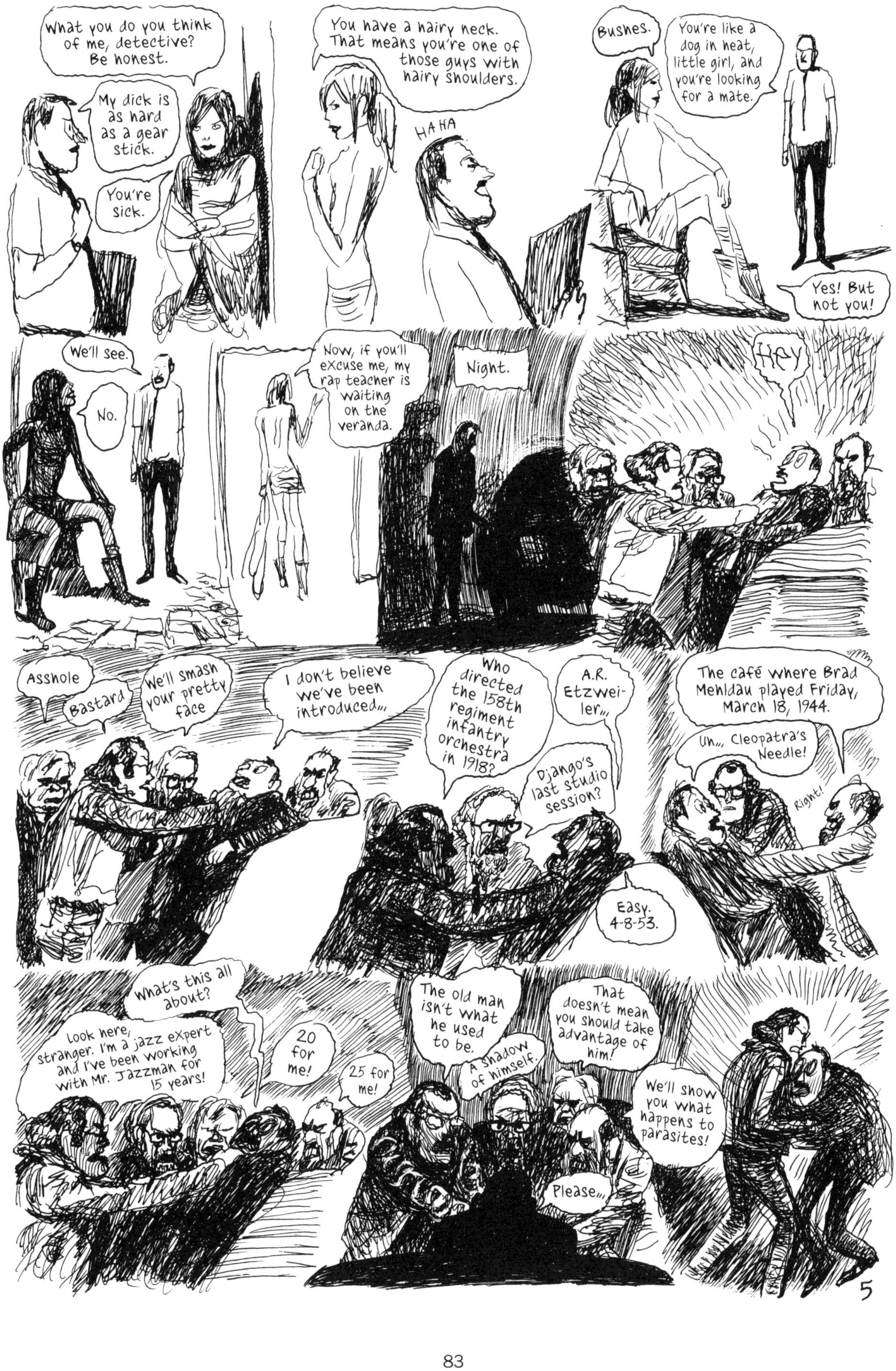
What you do you think of me, detective? Be honest.
My dick is as hard as a gear stick.
You're sick.
You have a hairy neck. That means you're one of those guys with hairy shoulders.
HAHA
Bushes.
You're like a dog in heat, little girl, and you're looking for a mate.
Yes! But not you!
We'll see.
No.
Now, if you'll excuse me, my rap teacher is waiting on the veranda.
Night.
Hey
Asshole
Bastard
We'll smash your pretty face
I don't believe we've been introduced...
Who directed the 158th regiment infantry orchestra in 1918?
A.R. Etzweiler...
Django's last studio session?
Easy. 4-8-53.
The café where Brad Mehldau played Friday, March 18, 1944.
Uh... Cleopatra's Needle!
Right!
What's this all about?
Look here, stranger. I'm a jazz expert and I've been working with Mr. Jazzman for 15 years!
20 for me!
25 for me!
The old man isn't what he used to be.
A shadow of himself.
That doesn't mean you should take advantage of him!
We'll show you what happens to parasites!
Please...
5

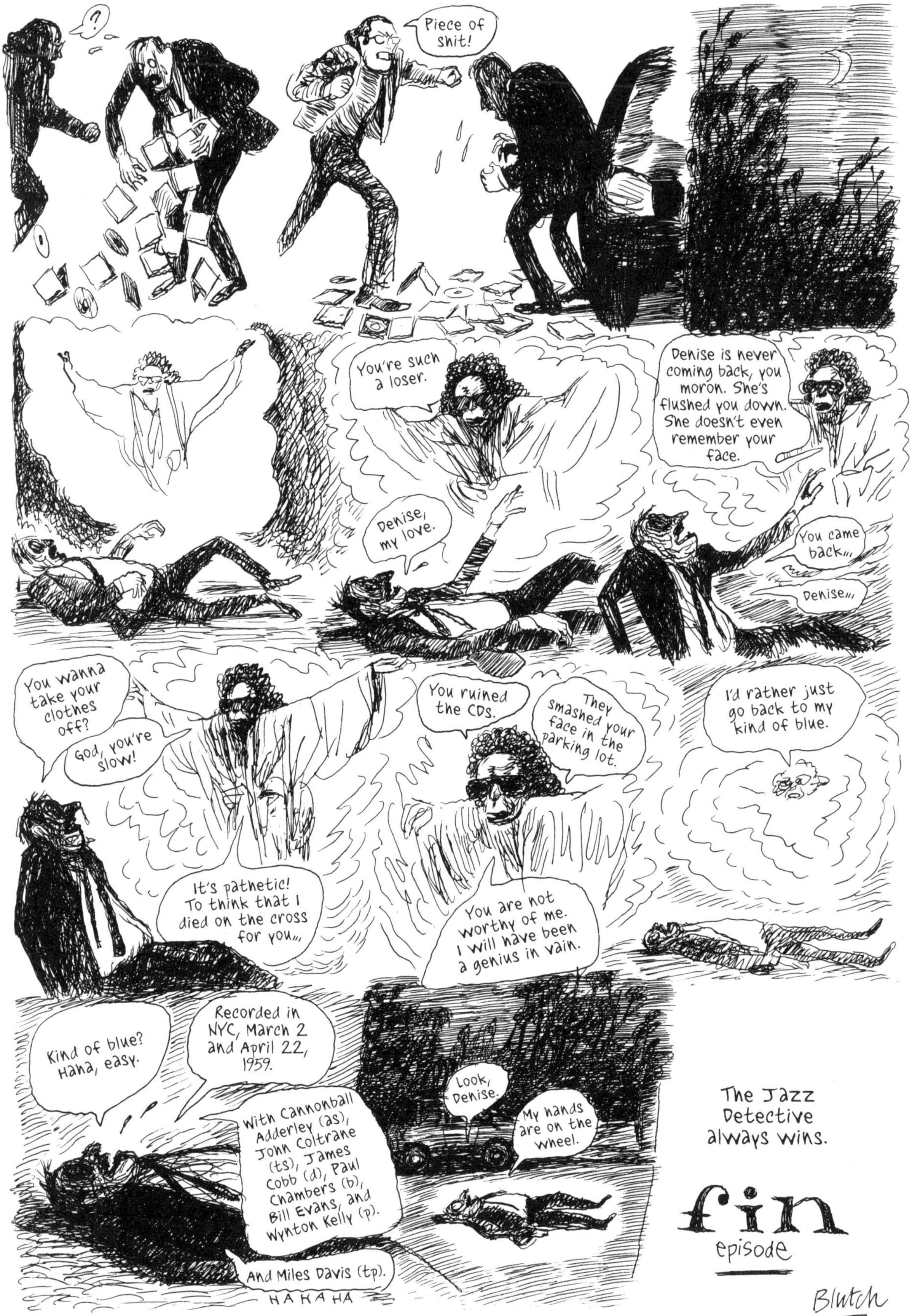

?
Piece of shit!
You're such a loser.
Denise is never coming back, you moron. She's flushed you down. She doesn't even remember your face.
Denise, my love.
You came back...
Denise...
You wanna take your clothes off?
God, you're slow!
It's pathetic! To think that I died on the cross for you...
You ruined the CDs.
They smashed your face in the parking lot.
You are not worthy of me. I will have been a genius in vain.
I'd rather just go back to my kind of blue.
Kind of blue? Haha, easy.
Recorded in NYC, March 2 and April 22, 1959.
With Cannonball Adderley (as), John Coltrane (ts), James Cobb (d), Paul Chambers (b), Bill Evans, and Wynton Kelly (p).
And Miles Davis (tp).
HAHAHA
Look, Denise.
My hands are on the wheel.
The Jazz Detective always wins.
fin
episode
Blutch

epilogue

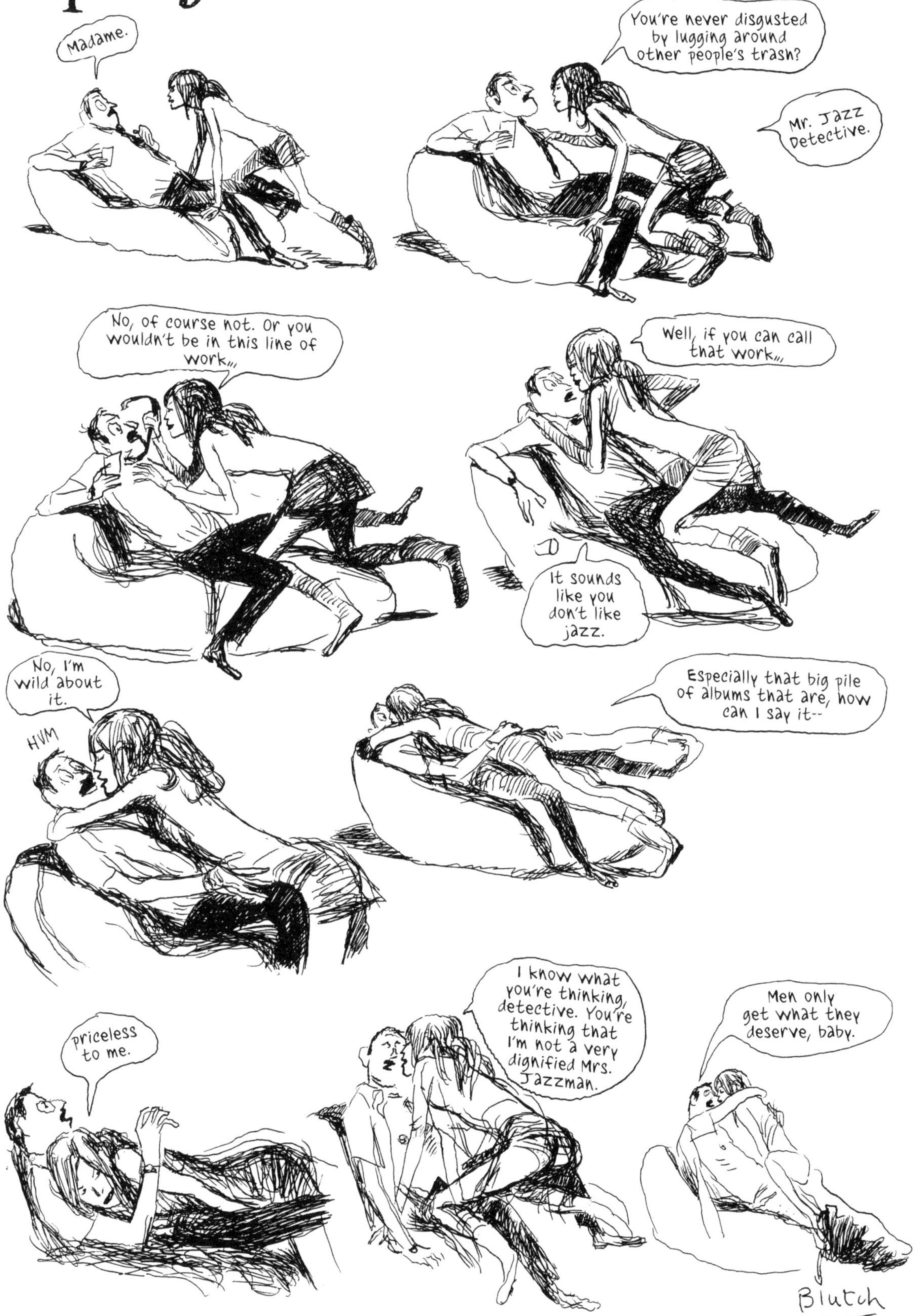
Madame.
You're never disgusted by lugging around other people's trash?
Mr. Jazz Detective.
No, of course not. Or you wouldn't be in this line of work,,,
Well, if you can call that work,,,
It sounds like you don't like jazz.
No, I'm wild about it.
HVM
Especially that big pile of albums that are, how can I say it--
priceless to me.
I know what you're thinking, detective. You're thinking that I'm not a very dignified Mrs. Jazzman.
Men only get what they deserve, baby.
Blutch

BLUTCH ON JAZZ

And the Making of *Total Jazz*

Interview by Michael Patin

From *Jazz News*

Could anyone imagine a better remedy for the post-election hangover than an hour in the company of Blutch on the sun-soaked terrace of his Lilas apartment on Monday, April 24 [2017]?[1] Thirty years after his first publication, everyone agrees that he should be considered a master of contemporary comics. Except the man himself, who knows nothing else but to plunge himself into a state of permanent questioning — without which his aura would not be the same. Lulled by his soft voice and struck by his demanding intellect, it would be easy to trace each convolution of his artistic journey with him, from *Mademoiselle Sunnymoon* (1993) to *Vitesse Moderne*[2] (2002), from *Péplum*[3] (1998) to *La Volupté* (2006), from *Petit Christian* (1998 and 2008) to *Pour en finir avec le cinéma*[4] (2011) — and to lose oneself in the conversation until the end of the legislative elections.[5]

But we came here with one intention: to talk about jazz. The timing of the Banlieues Bleues Festival, for which he (once again) designed the poster, was an excuse to get together. Numerous readings of his masterpiece, the well-named *Total Jazz*, served as his credentials. (Blutch is not content with feeding his obsessions to find refuge in them.) Following is a dialogue with an artist who discovered how to "translate the untranslatable" through the power of his graphic language.

For several years now, you have designed the poster for the Banlieues Bleues Festival.

It's been five or six years that I've been working with Xavier Lemaître and his team. I don't really keep track. I have a lot of appreciation for them and this festival.

Before that, you collaborated with *Jazzman* magazine.

I was contacted back then—about twenty years ago—by Alex Dutilh. Before becoming a good friend of mine, he was someone who had influenced me a lot without my realizing it because I listened to his radio programs on jazz when I was young. He participated in shaping my tastes in jazz to a certain extent. From 2000 to 2004, I drew pages and a few covers for his magazine—now defunct.

Pages that were compiled for *Total Jazz*.[6] In the preface, you explain that you were, at the time, sick of jazz.

I'd had enough of having to work on the subject every month. It's a rough pace to work at because you'd think you'd have plenty of time, but, really, no. After a while, pleasure became work, drudgery. I felt like I was doing homework.

Isn't it always like that when you get absorbed in a passion?

In the beginning, I had a really precise ambition. I wanted to translate the untranslatable, to move the abstract and ineffable side of music into the concrete form of drawing. I had given myself a problem to solve, like ones you give to children in school—all the while knowing, vaguely, that the problem would remain unsolved after many reflections and doubts. The problem is that music gives me a break from my work. It leads me to other emotions, ones I can't produce, having no musical training whatsoever. In making music a subject for work, I simplified it. Even when we represent musicians physically, we simplify them. They're sealed in a bottle, pinned like butterflies, and they lose their liberty and mystery.

---

1   The first round of the French presidential elections took place on April 23, 2017.

2   Published as *Modern Speed* in English by Europe Comics in 2017.

3   Published as *Peplum* in English by New York Review Comics in 2016.

4   Published as *So Long, Silver Screen* in English by PictureBox in 2013 and Europe Comics in 2017.

5   The legislative elections for the French National Assembly took place June 11 and 18, 2017.

6   Published by Seuil in 2004 and re-edited in an augmented version by Cornelius in 2013.

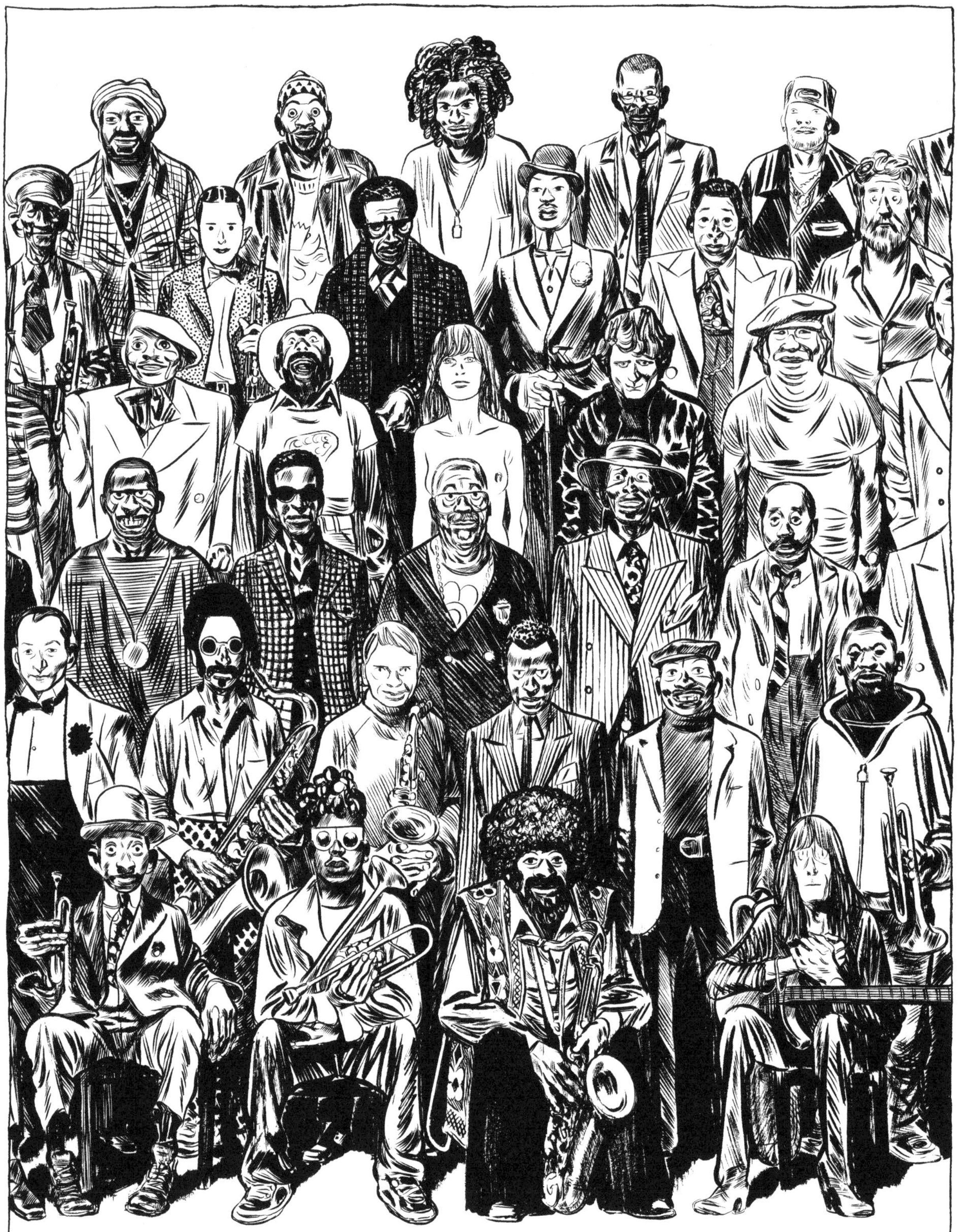
Blutch

Blutch's drawing for the Banlieues Bleues Jazz Festival poster referred to in the interview.

Translate the untranslatable: that includes the representation of sound, a recurrent element in *Total Jazz*, from the first pages—those dedicated to Stan Getz or Wayne Shorter—all the way to the last ones, like "The Abstract Truth."

Yes, I finished by drawing lines on the paper. *Total Jazz* is a book that I love, but after four years, I felt burned out. And that's not at all the case today. Music once again became an inexhaustible source of joy. I remember that in 2002, after the first round of the presidential election, we were shocked and sickened. For two weeks, I listened to Léo Ferré, because his anger consoled me.

What were your entry points into jazz? The page "Jazz in the Middle Ages" reveals a child misunderstood by his family because he listens to Coltrane; is it inspired by a real-life experience?

I remember listening to Coltrane on the record player in my father's living room when he got home from work in the evenings, [and him] not really wanting to listen to that.

How do you discover Coltrane at that age when you don't have parents that are into jazz?

Thanks to Alex Dutilh and the radio. I clearly remember a series of broadcasts he did on Coltrane. The other entry point was cinema. There was a film that I thoroughly enjoyed and that I haven't seen since—it's probably pretty mediocre—it's *The Glenn Miller Story* by Anthony Mann,[7] whose original soundtrack I bought. There was also the music of Duke Ellington for *Anatomy of a Murder* and the soundtrack for *Elevator to the Gallows* by Miles Davis. And Cassavetes in the television series *Johnny Staccato*.[8] I learned a lot about jazz through image.

You can feel this influence from cinema in the way in which you treat music, especially in the representation of the musicians.

Yes, because they're beautiful, much more beautiful than the actors, I think. They are "above-actors," more successful than some Hollywood stars. That's the other reason why I wanted to do a comic about jazz. Their charisma, their strength, their roughness, are very photogenic. As a comics artist, it's hard to resist that.

You mentioned Ferré a minute ago; did he also make that connection for you?

It's all connected for me. Ferré, it's about free jazz in his way of approaching text and song. He composed disheveled suites that lasted eighteen or twenty minutes. Poetry, literature, jazz—it all fits together.

Comics, through their history and notably in [the magazine] *Fluide Glacial*, who you've worked closely with, have always been associated more with rock than with jazz.

It's true, and, what's more, I really grew up in this atmosphere because I subscribed to *Métal Hurlant*[9] in the early '80s. There was *Les Enfants du Rock*,[10] Manœuvre,[11] Dionnet,[12] rock comics. All my friends were in rock groups and wanted to become famous. But this difference between us never bothered me.

In the last story of *Total Jazz* (to end with jazz), there is this character, the jazz detective, who represents collectors who know everything about their subject. Was this a way to sort of make fun of specialists and maybe even your own obsessions?

Collecting and amassing covers of Camembert containers, that feels a bit too "reclusive hoarder." But it's still a thing for those guys who don't manage to grow up. At the same time, when I'm interested in a musician, I want to know everything, all the way into the least respectable parts of their discography. I became a collector without necessarily wanting to. Today, all my rows of CDs make my seventeen-year-old son laugh.

Do you manage to be as passionate about contemporary musicians?

There's a lot of guys that I appreciate. The problem is that I always tell myself they're going to disappoint me the next time! I really loved the triple album by Kamasi Washington, that has a sense of both enthusiasm and density at the same time. In another genre, I quite like Christian Scott.

---

7   *Romance inachevée* in the French version.
8   He was appropriated as a character in *Fluide Glacial*.
9   Literally "Screaming Metal" but translated as *Heavy Metal* when published in America (1977).
10   Literally, "The Children of Rock"—an '80s television show on pop culture.
11   Philippe Manœvre, editor-in-chief for *Métal Hurlant*, writer and later editor for *Rock & Folk*, and host of an '80s television show on French rock, *Les Grandes Manœuvres*.
12   Jean-Pierre Dionnet, co-founder and editor-in-chief of *Métal Hurlant*.

I also listen to the old guys who still record today, like pianist Stanley Cowell, or Dave Brubeck when he recorded solo versions of the songs from his youth. The hoary artists move me.

Do you also go to concerts?

I have a lot fewer opportunities to go. For me, it's not at all the same. Like, right now, I'm listening to a lot of Cannonball Adderley while drawing. His studio albums are amazing, but his live albums are even better. Incidentally, I think that the best moment in all of Clint Eastwood's films is in *Play Misty for Me*, his directorial debut, when he's filming a Cannonball Adderley concert. I think about it a lot.

Do you see a link between your approach to comics and the process of playing jazz? I'm thinking specifically about covering songs, drawing known characters as standards adapt.

I always do that. Right now, I'm working on an album in which I take passages from comics that I like, reassembled on the same page. I just finished the twenty-third page:

there's Hergé, Graton, Jacques Martin, Pétillon, Franquin, Morris, Giraud, Crepax, Gillon, Lauzier, Gotlib… It's called *Variations*, and that's already a musical title. For me, jazz is always waiting in ambush; it's a continual source of inspiration.

In an interview for *Le Temps*, you said that Wayne Shorter or Herbie Hancock influenced you more than Hergé or Franquin, because you could never love the same character for several decades.

It's true. For me, work is a perpetual challenge. I couldn't have limited myself to the same motif for years, the process we coarsely call a "career." This year marks thirty years since I published my first comic. And the more I advance, the less I understand what it is. This "cover album" (*Variations*) is a way to ask myself what I'm doing, what I devoted my life to, what is the point of this whole undertaking. It's also to rediscover the childlike pleasure of drawing, like when I used to copy Donald [Duck] and Astérix. I feel like I'm coming back towards a primal scream.

Christian Hincker, better known by his pseudonym
Blutch, is a French cartoonist who has been a prominent
figure in European comics since the late 1980s. Known
for his scratchy pen-and-pencil drawings and masterful
storytelling, Blutch won the 2009 Grand Prize at Angoulême
International Comics Festival. Blutch also cowrote and
codirected the animated film *Fear[s] of the Dark*.

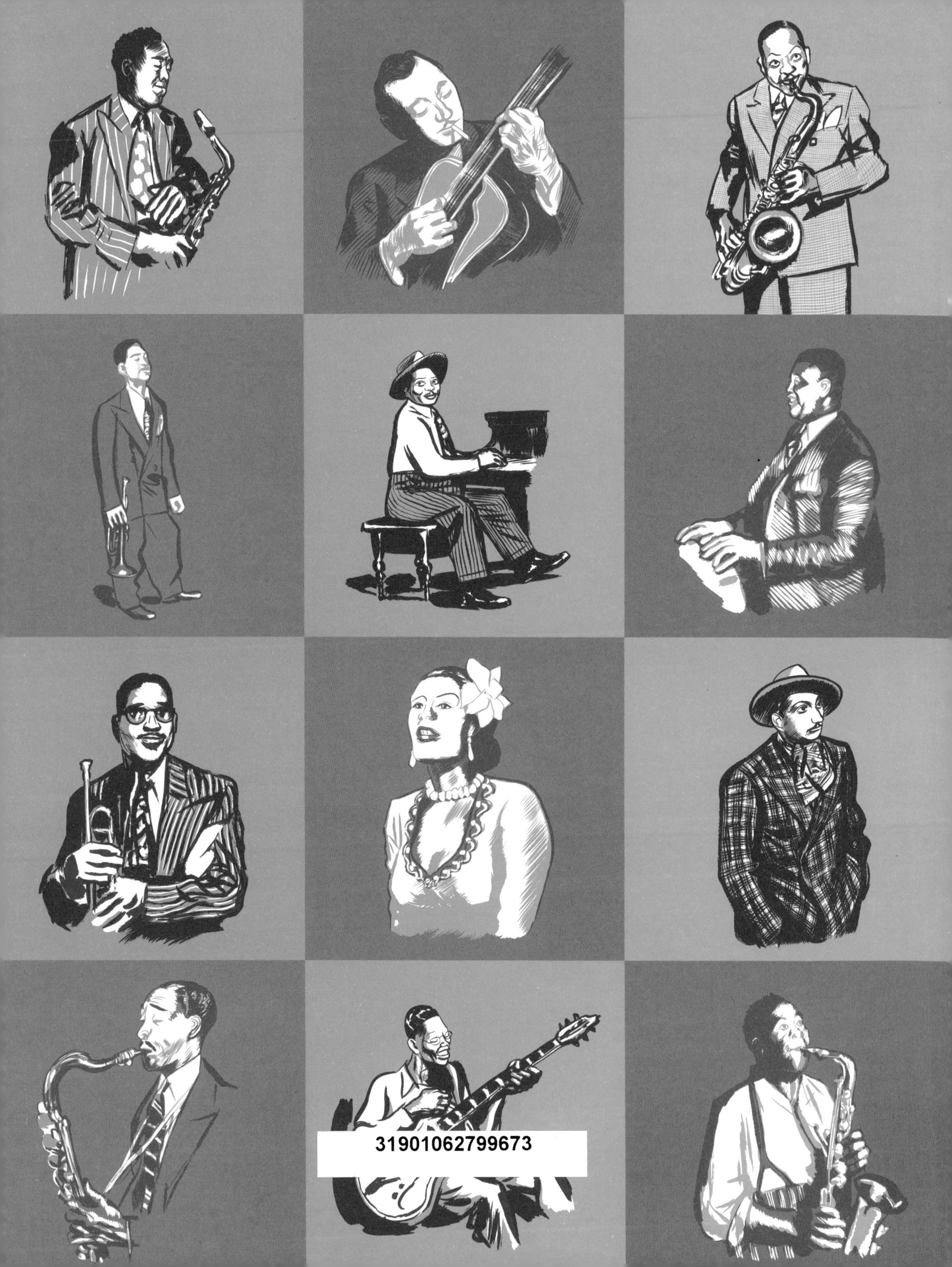